I0519560

Magic?

by

Art Bell

ISBN-10: 1-947373-26-9

ISBN-13: 978-1-947373-26-6

Printed in the United States of America

Deposited in the Library of Congress

First Edition

Lexingford Publishing LLC
Los Angeles   New York   Hong Kong
www.lexingfordpublishingllc.com

Chapter One
Three Ships

"Journal it. You'll feel better."

That was the advice from my Boston College English professor when, in office hours, I began telling her my earthshaking personal story. It's taken me several years and more than one new printer cartridge, but I've followed her suggestion/put-off. I have journaled it. Now it is out of my hair and into yours. BTW, I don't feel better yet.

We begin, of course, with me—Tom. Picture me, as you must, at 19, a college freshman, average in height/weight/looks/number of friends (about five, depending on the day). In truth, I probably have one toe on the Asperger's spectrum in that I tend to obsess on tasks, even unappealing ones.

Take my finances (please). I'm on a budget, one target of my obsession. I call my parents toward the end of every month to make sure they have transferred my "allowance" (a word that makes me feel about ten years old) into my college bank account. They've never failed to do so, but I worry about being broke. One toe, maybe two on the spectrum.

What is unique about me is that I can move things. To be clear, I'm not talking about Two-College-Guys-with-a-Truck moving services. I can move small things by looking at them and willing them to move.

Let me qualify that claim. I can't move things with any particular amount of weight to them—say, a penny. I can stare at a penny, willing it to move with all my might, and nada. It obeys Newton, not me.

Even more problematic for me is the episodic nature of my unique skill: I can't make my mental moving skills happen on command. A couple times I caught good videos of my performance on my iPhone. The videos show me, the table, the objects moving. In fact, I once submitted a proposal to demonstrate my abilities at my Senior Science Fair. But they rejected me, based on the arguable notion that science has to be repeatable to be true. I can't guarantee if or when my unique skill is going to do its thing.

But rewind for a moment. What can I move? Since discovering my ability at age fifteen and learning to call it psychokinesis, I've had my best (only) luck with little bits of paper folded in half and placed on edge, like the letter "A" without the crossbar. These are my little ships, as I think of them. I typically place three on a glass table-top— a polished tabletop also suffices—and I will them to move toward me. By "will them," I mean precisely what you would expect: focusing on them and mentally commanding/coaxing/cajoling/cussing at them to slide on over. They do so about ten percent of the time. Don't ask me why. I don't know.

My greatest successes have come when all my little paper ships move in concert, like the Nina, Pinta, and Santa Maria. Slowly but surely, they scoot a foot or two toward me before stopping dead in their tracks. My most frequent failures have come when I've tried to show this "trick," as he insists on calling it, to my skeptical roommate, Johnson.

"So, go ahead," he told me the third week of our first semester. "I'm watching."

I had casually mentioned that I could make a little piece of paper move across my desk without touching it. He bet me a six-pack (beer, not abs) that I couldn't.

I prepped one little paper ship as usual and set it out about 18 inches from me on the clean, smooth surface of my desk. Having any clean surface for my activity was a rare phenomenon in our pigsty of a dorm room. Johnson's fault, not mine.

"And?" Johnson prompted.

"Be quiet," I told him. "Let me focus." I stared intensely at the tiny piece of paper and mentally urged it to move.

"I think I saw something," Johnson murmured. "Your head moved closer to the piece of paper. Technically, you closed the distance by an inch or two."

"Shut up," I snapped. "I can do this. Just watch." I bore down, sending laser beam commands from my mind— MOVE, goddamn you!—to the piece of paper mocking me on the desk. Nothing. Not even a shiver of movement.

"Maybe I should blow on it to get it started," Johnson quipped. "That's what she said." He snickered.

I told him to fuck himself and just watch. I put my fingers to my temples, closed my eyes, and tried with all my might to either make the paper move or give myself a brain hemorrhage. Still nothing.

Johnson grabbed his jacket. "It's been real," he laughed. "Well, not real, actually. Kind of pretend." He was still chuckling to himself as he left the room, probably on the way to cafeteria to regale a knot of our mutual friends with what he had just witnessed (or not).

I flopped back in my chair and, in disgust, gave the finger to my failure-to-launch slip of paper. And, of course, then it moved. As if drawn by some invisible thread, it slid obediently toward me, stopping at the edge of the desk. "Just a couple minutes late, you stupid piece of shit," I hissed, wadding up the paper slip and tossing it in the general direction of the waste can near the door.

I mention this incident not only to introduce you to Johnson, who will play a surprising role later in my story, but also to demonstrate my dilemma. I possess a skill— who knows, perhaps the first human being ever to have it—that insists on blowing hot and cold (mostly cold) in my demo efforts for others.

On the occasions when a little paper ship cooperated, it would often move an inch or so, then stop dead. "Did you see that?" I asked onlookers. "See what?" was the usual response. "It moved," I protested. The sniggles would begin: "Yeah, when the door opened" or "When you sneezed" or "I didn't see anything. Do it again right now."

Within my first month in college, I was getting strange looks from people I didn't even know. Perhaps they were saying to themselves, "That's the kid who thinks he can make things move." For the sake of some semblance of a social life, I shelved my psychokinetic demonstrations, or at least reserved them for my own amusement when I was alone.

On balance, I estimate that I succeeded in getting the piece of paper to move, sometimes an inch, sometimes a yard, only about once in 10 attempts or so. Believe me, I have charted all possible variables—time of day, weather, my own energy or fatigue level, the brand of paper involved, the question of open-eyes or closed-eyes, and many other factors. Nothing explained my frequent failure to launch or my occasional successes.

But I did know one thing: the occasional, unexplained good luck I had in moving a piece of paper always filled me with feelings of awe, bewilderment, and something akin to "superpowers" from the comic books. I would shout "Yes!" or something more dramatic—"Fucking A!"—or "Mazel tov" for the two Jewish guys on my floor--in the vain hope that someone, anyone, would come over, observe my triumph, and pat me on the back as the one-in-107-billion humans who have lived on Earth (I looked it up) possessing genuine psychokinetic powers.

By my third month in college I had lived down the stigma of "Movement Man," as Johnson persisted in calling me. There were other interests to pursue, above all joining the general stampede of my classmates to get into one another's pants. Johnson, to his credit, was helpful in this regard.

"I know this girl named Viola from my Biology class," he confided over a late-night beerfest in the dorm. "You should meet her."

"Viola? Like the instrument?" I replied.

He gave me a blank stare. "Viola, like in my Biology class," he repeated. "She's reasonably hot and, as far as I can tell, not too picky about who she hooks up with."

"Thanks a lot," I shot back, reaching for something to throw at him.

"But, dude," he continued, "you've got to quit that weird shit." He pointed toward my desk where three tiny paper ships sat motionless. I had forgotten to throw them away. "That make-it-move crap is going to scare away any girl. Even Viola."

I nodded and swept the paper bits off my desk. "And I meet this stellar beauty how?"

Johnson already had a plan. "I know where she eats lunch. Tomorrow we'll sit down next to her and you can ask her if she wants to go out for a drink or something." He made a socking motion with his fist, vaguely suggesting 'putting it to her,' I guessed.

I hadn't had sex—at least, with a living, breathing girl— since my senior prom in high school. I was, as they say in baseball, "due." We high-fived each other on the lunch plan.

The next day Johnson met me in the food line. He pointed behind his hand at a girl sitting by herself at a nearby table. Her back was toward us. "Was I right?" Johnson prodded. I could see long, dark hair, a hang-loose sweater, and black tights of some kind. There were obscure outlines of a body inside this outfit. Some version of a body was a minimal requirement for sexual involvement, I felt, although my criteria in this regard were broad indeed.

We took our trays and made our way in her direction through the crowded cafeteria. I was wearing a clean shirt with a collar—a collar, for God's sake, practically the tuxedo of college life. Johnson was moving quickly toward Viola. I grabbed his sleeve to slow him down. His metaphoric ass wasn't on the line here. I was the one who was apparently going to blurt out those risky words inviting her to join me for a drink, and possibly more.

I hung back a step and two and watched Johnson set his tray across from Viola at the table. She seemed to recognize him. The first words I heard her say to Johnson were "yeah, Biology. Right."

I took a breath and sat down between Johnson and the raven-tressed Viola. I blurted out my name, hard for those of us teetering on the spectrum, and heard her say "Vi." Self-introductions are ridiculously self-conscious for nineteen-year-olds. There's no shaking of hands or "nice to meet you" banter. It's just your name, with the silent, fervent hope that she caught it the first time and wouldn't make me repeat it. Or, worse, say "what was your name?" ten minutes into the conversation.

"So," she said, looking up from her salad. As Johnson had claimed, she was quite attractive. "What are you guys doing today?"

Johnson made up some incoherent bullshit about the many hours lying ahead of him in the library. He stopped

10

in mid-sentence, expecting me to take over. "But Tom here—" He let the words hang in the air.

"Uh . . . today," I mumbled. "Well, today I'm basically doing nothing." Sometimes the truth is the best lie.

"Me, too," she volunteered, and went back to munching her salad. Johnson nudged me hard under the table.

"We just met," I began, saying the words too quietly for any human ear to perceive. Another painful nudge from Johnson. "Viola—Vi--"

She looked up. "How did you know my name was Viola? I just said Vi." She was curious.

"He told me," I answered, nodding toward Johnson. "And there aren't too many other names that could have 'Vi' as a nickname, right? Maybe Viagra." I thought it was funny. I could feel Johnson dying inside.

"What?" she frowned, looking first at me and then at Johnson. I knew better than to repeat the Viagra bit. I noticed a small tattoo on the inside of her wrist—the name 'Roy' in fading script.

"Actually, Vi," I started again, feeling a mini-surge of testosterone triggered by my apparent competition, Roy. "Tonight around 8, Johnson and I are going to have a beer and some wings at that place, what's-its-name . . ."

"The Dive," she helped out. "It's called the Dive."

"Yeah, well, if you want to come with us, we could meet you there." I was looking down, the favorite direction for Asperger wanna-not-be's. I vaguely heard Johnson protesting about an overdue report and his decision to stay in the library until it was done.

"I guess it's just you and me," Vi said nonchalantly, picking up her tray. "See you there at 8 or so."

When she was out of sight, Johnson pretended to mop his brow. "You are a complete asshole," he whispered hoarsely. "What's this 'Johnson and I' crap? That wasn't the deal."

"OK, OK," I held up my palms. "I was nervous. I thought she would laugh in my face if I asked her out of my own. Besides, she seemed to like you better."

Exasperated, Johnson picked up his tray. "She knows me. She just met you." He turned away from the table, then shot back over his shoulder, "8 pm at the Dive. You and her—alone! And don't bring any fucking bits of paper!"

I wandered around campus for about an hour, aiming for that purposeful stride that freshmen take on when they don't know where the hell they're going. Eventually, I landed back in my room by noon. I sprawled out on my bed and thought about Vi's dark eyes and straight-forward manner. Then, God help me, I wondered if she would be interested in my psychokinetic powers, if I could actually make them happen for her. It was a powerful cocktail: the prospect of eventual sex with Vi and the equally heady scenario of showing her my stuff in the form of little paper ships coursing across the bar table at the Dive, utterly and unexplainably compliant to my will. 'Oh, Tom,' I could almost hear Vi exclaiming, 'that is so cool. Take me now!'

I fell asleep for a couple hours, then showered in preparation for my first semi-real date in college. I passed on the three collared shirts I owned--dorky, I felt—and grabbed a pair of jeans that were mid-way between tight and baggy. Ditto with the sweatshirt I found at the bottom of a yet-unpacked cardboard box from home. It bore the slogan "Don't You Dare," which I thought would be a provocative conversation-starter with Vi. 'Don't You Dare' what? Resist my attractions? Try to pick up the check? Tell anyone about the erotic adventures of our yet-to-arrive sex life? Ask me how I made those pieces of paper move?

Oops, there's that intrusive obsession again--the psychokinetic powers that distinguish me from anyone Vi has ever met or will ever meet, including Roy. But who knows, maybe she will be interested. And maybe my powers won't let me down.

At quarter to 8, I headed to the Dive, having unconsciously tucked a couple little pieces of paper into a back pocket of my jeans. I had to let my eyes adjust to the dim, smoky haze inside the bar. To my amazement and my delight, Vi had already arrived. There she was, wearing somewhat different clothes than at lunch. The tights looked the same, but her top was one of those combination affairs, with a loose blouse slipped off one shoulder. revealing a black bra strap. It was "the look" for night outings at college, I knew.

What I hadn't expected were the two guys already buzzing around her table. They were loud and she was giggling. She already had a bottle of beer in front of her, along with a basket of wings. Had the two intruders plied her with this food? Was one of these fuckers Roy? And what would they say if I made a piece of paper move across the table right in front of their eyes? What do you say now, big guys?

I shook off the thought and approached the table—the throne, as it were—with my best imitation of careless bravado. Vi looked over. "Hey, Tom!" Good start. She remembered my name. I pulled up a chair, smiled, and sat down. The other two guys sauntered off in search of greener pastures.

I couldn't help it. "I thought we said 8 o'clock," I blurted out, glancing at my cellphone for the exact time. A plan is a plan and time exists for a reason: to keep us on schedule. The event horizon moves on inexorably and didn't abide sloppiness in arrivals or departures. I could feel the tingle of Asperger's telling me 'why the hell did she get here so early?' At the same time, the brake pedal of rationality screamed the counter-message: 'what the hell does it matter when she arrived?'

Vi looked momentarily confused, but then just answered my stupid question: "I was bored. And hungry. So, I came over here about an hour ago."

An hour ago? OMG, this lady crosses all the red lines of plans, schedules, agreements, and probably international treaties. "Yeah," I mumbled, "good idea. I mean, why be bored in your room, and hungry, too, when you can just come over to the Dive, like, 60 minutes early? Wow, 60 minutes."

"Do you want some wings?" she offered. "I already ate half of them. I'm stuffed." She took a long swig of beer. Using my fake ID for the first time off campus, I waved at the server and got two more beers for the table.

Vi laughed. "Well, this makes my third. I had two before you got here."

I laughed back in her same pitch. "Three beers! I've got some catching up to do."

Thank you, Jesus, she was a talker. Time flew by as she unburdened herself of every frustration brought into her life by her roommate ("Big Alice"), her parents (who didn't let her choose the college she wanted to attend), her former boyfriend, Roy, who didn't go to college at all and at least could have the courtesy to call her once, just as a friend, to see how she was doing in a new city . . . and she was getting his tattooed name erased if it didn't hurt . . . ET CETERA, writ large. Lots of et cetera.

I provided the requisite nodding and "so true's" and "you're kidding's." She asked me a few questions along the lines of "Don't you think so?" Of course, I said yes, I really thought so, absolutely, Vi. After five or six beers— we began to lose count—her eyes looked dreamy and her blitz of conversation slowed considerably. We were leaning closer to one another.

"I've got a secret," she whispered. She cupped her hand around my cheek, then realized she had missed my ear. She tried again. "I'm wasted," she rasped.

"Oh, *really*?" I replied, with what I thought was a good blend of mild surprise mixed with the anticipation of scoring.

"Yeah, the only good thing about my roommate Big Alice is that she has a Big Stash of really quality weed." Vi was quiet for a moment, probably listening to her own words bounce around in her head. "So, she and I got high before I came over here."

"Nice way to spend an afternoon," I whispered back. "Do you want to get out of here?"

I didn't realize that those words—I got them from the movies--had such powerful code connotations. She grabbed my arm, murmured "definitely," and tried to stand up.

I reached in my back pocket for my wallet to pay for the beers and wings. My little pieces of paper fluttered out onto the table. She pounced like a cat: "What are these?" She pinched one of the paper bits between her fingers. I think she had visions of rolling a joint right there on the spot.

"Nothing," I said. "Paper. Just . . . well, nothing."

She wouldn't let it go. "Why do you carry little pieces of paper?" Her legs were wobbly, but her wits weren't.

"I--" Big decision time. Is she really interested in the fact that she is about to hook up with the only living or dead TRUE psychokineticist in the history of the fucking world? "Vi, sit down again." I cleared a swath across the table. "Do you want to see something interesting?"

She nodded. That was enough for me. It had been a long time--even longer than my sex hiatus--since someone had indicated any sincere interest in my special talent.

"OK," I said. "Let's take these three ordinary bits of paper." I placed them all in her palm and asked her to assure herself that they were just ordinary paper, not magnetic strips or something from a magician's toolkit. "Now we'll fold them like this." I made my three little A-shaped ships and set them across the table from the two of us. She watched intently. Was she truly interested or just in a THC-induced stupor. I chose to believe she was watching me.

"I don't want this to sound like bragging," I began. "But when I was fifteen or so I discovered that I could make little things move using only the power of my mind."

"The power of your mind . . ." she said, trying hard to focus. She squinted her eyes.

"It doesn't always work. Sometimes—in fact, often—the bits of paper just sit there and I feel like an idiot."

"An idiot . . ." she repeated, coming in and out of her haze.

"But, when it does work, it's glorious. Maybe the greatest single advancement in human powers in the last 50,000 years." I made up the 50,000 years part. I think it is probably more. Depends if you count Neanderthals or Samovians. All right, Asperger's redivivus.

"Are you ready?" I asked. She nodded and started to get to her feet, as if we were leaving the Dive. "No, I mean are you ready to see these three little pieces of paper cross this table, drawn only by the power of my mind?"

She plopped back down, grasping my general drift. "OK, I'm ready," she purred. She rested her chin in both hands and stared at my bits of paper across the table.

I concentrated my mind on moving the ships toward us. I knew full well that it didn't matter whether I focused intently or not. Sometimes they moved toward me when I least expected it. At other times, it took a prolonged sweat of effort to get them to budge. And usually it didn't happen at all.

"Nothing's happening," she said.

"Yes, I can tell that," I replied, trying hard to hide my growing exasperation while still conjuring my powers, such as they were. "Just keep watching the three little ships."

"I thought they were bits of paper," she mumbled.

"OK, I just call them little ships because that's sort of what they look like to me when they travel across the table."

She wasn't satisfied. "They don't look like ships to me. Why don't you just use pennies?"

I felt myself losing patience, even on a first date. "Vi, pennies weigh much, much more than these little pieces of paper. Pennies would be extremely hard to move. No one can move pennies, for god's sake."

"I can move pennies." She was being playful. She grabbed a few coins from her pocket and moved two of them in circles around the table. "See?"

"Yes, I see your pennies. But don't touch them. Just make them move using your mind." I looked at her seriously. She wasn't as wasted as she pretended.

"Well, that would be impossible," she said in a classroom voice. "Things don't move because we just think about them."

"Watch," I said, taking up the challenge. Miraculously, inexplicably, the three little ships decided to cooperate at that moment. In short bursts of motion, an inch or two at a time, they each moved slowly across the width of the tabletop, one getting ahead of the other. Within a matter of seconds, they lay still right in front of us at the edge of the table.

I looked at Vi for her reaction. She was silent for a long moment. Finally, she spoke: "They are so cute. And they do look a little like ships."

"But, Vi," I protested, "do you realize what you just saw? No one touched those bits of paper. They moved across this table"—I knocked on the wood tabletop for emphasis—"just because my mind told them to."

"And do you know what my mind is telling me right now?" she breathed. "I would love to hook up with someone—in fact, someone exactly like you." Her hand inadvertently swept the little ships off the table and onto the floor. Jesus, Vi, my ships!

I glanced around in the vain hope that someone else had been looking over our shoulders and had seen what I had done. No such luck. There were people at surrounding tables, but they were deep into their booze and one another.

As we left the Dive and headed toward my room, which Johnson had conveniently vacated for the night, I felt twin tsunamis of emotion washing over me. On one hand, here was Vi, not only willing but leading the way to a night of sexual adventure. On the other hand, here was my semi-sober witness to one of the greatest events in human history. Would she stop right in the middle of making love to say, "Wait. What about those little ships? How in the hell did you do that? You are amazing, Tom!"

I fervently hoped so. Maybe I would demonstrate the feat again, right there on my bed and right on the spot, although wrinkled sheets probably aren't the ideal surface for the movement of mind-propelled objects.

Or I might say, "Hold that thought."

Chapter Two
Cosmo and Me

Flash forward to the end of my freshman year in college. I'm sitting, reluctantly, in a physics seminar I took with the specific aim of demonstrating my psychokinetic abilities to someone, particularly my professor, who was neither a psychic believer nor a target of my affections.

My professor is 40-something, which he obviously considers to be very young indeed. "Call me Cosmo," he told us on the first day of class. "And I will call you by your first name." Most of us had trouble choking out "Cosmo" in class discussion with this guy. We slipped easily into the default of calling him "professor" or "doctor." He invariably corrected us: "Cosmo, remember?" Oy.

His seminar met once a week and was not popular with students. Even those who were physics majors (which I, emphatically, was not) disliked him. We had only seven students in our session. The prof (oops, Cosmo) had the maddening habit of starting class by attempting to springboard off whatever the previous professor in the room had written on the whiteboard. Because the class right before us was American history, Cosmo usually spent twenty minutes or so reaching for awkward, abstruse, and unlikely connections between national events past or present and some physical principle or property. He called it 'creative pedagogy.' We called it a waste of time and money.

"Franklin Delano Roosevelt," he read from the whiteboard. "What aspect of physics comes to mind when you think of FDR?"

All eyes fell in nauseous silence. We don't know. We don't care.

"Paralysis?" he ventured, hoping to stimulate conversation. "A wheelchair? Crutches?"

Still, no takers. Deathly silence.

"Well," he sighed. This was a welcome sign that he was ready to give up on class discussion. "I don't like to answer my own questions. But here's what I'm thinking."

Oh, God, this is painful. A mini-lecture on the stress points of wooden crutches and the physics of moving one's body weight (or, FDR's) in a wheelchair. Were we taking notes? No.

Cosmo liked to dismiss class on the early side, usually because he had run out of intellectual gas tackling American history references on the whiteboard through the lens of physics. Sometimes, perhaps out of guilt for ending class early, he turned to "open discussion" in which class members could discuss anything they wanted, so long as the topic related to physics, broadly defined.

"That's enough heavy lifting for today," he was saying. "Let's have open discussion." He sat cross-legged on the table at the head of class, looking at us, Yoda-like, over the rims of his glasses.

One of my frat brothers shot me a nasty glance, then asked Cosmo, "What do you think about psychokinesis?"

This stimulus was pedagogical cocaine for Cosmo. He turned pink and rubbed his hands, preparing to step into the batter's box and show us his swing.

"Psycho . . . kinEEsis, commonly known as PK," he entoned, struggling to contain his delight at getting something, anything, out of a student's mouth. A kiss-ass student, I thought.

He muddled through a handful of possibles for the PK throne: Uri Geller and spoonbending, Madame Palladino and table levitation, and the Great Kreskin. I had heard of the One Million Dollar Paranormal Prize offered by the James Randi Educational Foundation for any candidate who could demonstrate psychokinetic ability under scientific controls. The prize, Cosmo emphasized, has yet to be awarded.

My frat brother wouldn't give it a rest. "Tom has psychokinetic powers," he said evenly, as if it were accepted fact. I winced. Heads turned my way.

"Tom?" Cosmo's beady eyes found me. "Do you care to comment?"

I was tempted to just say no. But, I reminded myself, I was taking this stupid seminar for a moment like this. I screwed my courage to the sticking point (a phrase I learned in my Shakespeare class. I have no idea what it means.)

"I . . . I can sometimes make things move," I began.

Cosmo jumped in. "And haven't we all? We move our pens across paper. We move our furniture. We move our asses." Eyes shot up at the asses reference. Was he going really going there?

"I meant, movement using just my mind. The psycho part of psychokinesis," I clarified.

"Psycho," my frat brother whispered too loudly, pointing his finger toward me. I pointed back at him, using a different finger behind my hand.

"And what do you move with your mind?" Cosmo pursued.

I smiled, taking a breath. "Not much, really. I can't move anything very heavy, not even a penny. The only thing I can move—and it doesn't happen most of the time when I try—are small bits of paper. I make them move across a smooth surface."

"Interesting," Cosmo replied, with a hint of sarcasm. "And how many of you have observed Tom's ability in this regard?"

Two hands went up. Damn that fraternity.

"Tell me objectively what you saw Tom do," Cosmo prodded.

One of my so-called brothers took the bait. "I saw Tom lay out some little bits of paper on his desktop. He stared at them for a while and, sure enough, they slowly slid toward him, probably a couple feet or so."

"I saw the same thing," the other fink confirmed.

"Did you see this together?" Cosmo queried. The long arm of scientific investigation was reaching toward me.

"No," the two shook their heads. I don't remember showing my skills to either of them. Of course, memory is the first casualty of inebriated frat life.

Cosmo was already scribbling on the whiteboard. "Movement requires force in some form," he said, drawing unnecessary arrows pointing up, down, and sideways. "As you know from this class, we have four forces to choose from: the strong nuclear force, the weak nuclear force, the electromagnetic force binding electrons together, and gravitation."

For some reason, Cosmo felt compelled to write the forces on the board in large capital letters. "So, Tom, which force did you use to move your bits of paper?"

Got me. "I have no idea," I shrugged. "Those are the only forces to choose from?"

"All that we know of," Cosmo smirked. "Perhaps you used a fifth force. We could call it 'Tom's Force.'" He wrote that phrase on the whiteboard. The class laughed.

Cosmo proceeded to dash a formula onto the board, tapping each variable with his ring finger as he wrote. "BUT--" Cosmo liked to let this word hover. "Tom, how strong would Tom's Force have to be to overcome inertia and the electromagnetic force that requires those bits of paper to remain unmoved on your desk? Hmm?"

I wasn't looking up at him, knowing he would answer his own question if I held my tongue.

"Let me tell you." He inserted values for the variables in his formula on the board. *"Voila!* Q.E.D. The mysterious fifth force streaming out of your *incredible* mind"—he caught my eye in a mocking way—"would have to be A BILLION TIMES more powerful than any known force in order to make even the tiniest scrap of paper move even a millimeter." I flashed on a memory of Carl Sagan— BILLIONS AND BILLIONS.

Cosmo pointed to the mathematics scrawled on the board. "What do you have to say, Tom?"

Uh, maybe fuck you and the horse you rode in on, Cosmo? But I wanted to graduate. "I have no idea what forces are involved," I demurred, hoping to get out of this uncomfortable teaching moment with my dignity intact.

The frat bro sitting closest to me raised his hand. "Maybe Tom could show you what he does."

Cosmo seemed confused at the idea of observing any demonstration that he had not explained to himself beforehand. "Well?" he ventured.

My moment of truth, and my justification for registering for Cosmo's bullshit. "OK," I murmured, taking a piece of paper out of my notebook and clearing off the top of my desk. "I usually take two or three bits of paper." I tore off three postage-sized pieces of paper and began folding three little ships for their not-so-maiden voyage across the smooth desk surface.

"Hold on," Cosmo inserted, stepping toward me. "Do you see what's going on here? Tom, like any amateur magician, is choosing his own materials for this experiment. How do we know that the paper he is using does not contain iron filings that can be moved by a hidden magnet? Or perhaps he has used sleight of hand to connect an almost invisible thread to one or more of the pieces of paper. How else might Tom be deceiving us?"

The class was game for this hunt. "Maybe he uses puffs of air from his mouth or nose to move the paper bits." This from a girl in the back row who hadn't spoken all semester. The first puff of air from her mouth.

"Very good," responded Cosmo. Good for her, I thought, but bad for me. I had been tried and found guilty before my demonstration even began. So much for science.

"What other deceptions might Tom be using?" Cosmo wheedled. "Think like a cheater, not a scientist."

Another volunteer. "I've had bits of lint and other stuff jump around on my clothing due to static electricity. If he rubbed his sleeve over the desk, maybe a static charge could make the bits of paper move."

"Absolutely!" Cosmo crowed. "Or he may be tipping his desk slightly so that the bits of paper move a bit. But that's plain gravity at work, not any mysterious force from Tom's mind."

'Tom's mind' in the third person? Had I willed my brain to science? Was I not in the room? I proceeded in downcast silence to place my little folded paper ships at the edge of my desk. My voluble classmates gathered around my desk. Even Cosmo moved in for a close view.

"It doesn't always work," I muttered, trying to focus on the strenuous work of moving the paper bits. "Doesn't work most of the time."

The room fell completely silent. I concentrated. A minute, then another passed without result. You stubborn fuckers, I railed in my thoughts toward the unmoving ships. Not even a quiver of motion in the paper bits. Another couple minutes went by. I could feel myself starting to sweat. Who wouldn't sweat trying to generate A BILLION TIMES more force than the electromagnetism binding all the atoms in the universe together? You would and I did.

Cosmo let me dangle for perhaps five minutes. "I won't say Tom has failed," he pronounced, picking up the little paper ships from my desk as if they were dead roaches. "Perhaps we guessed his stratagem for moving the bits of paper and thereby foiled his demonstration?" He nodded a knowing 'yes' in my direction as he spoke.

"I told you it doesn't work most of the time," I protested to deaf ears all around.

"Re-PEAT-able!" Cosmo virtually shouted. "Tom, science depends on rePEATable observation. Only then can we say that phenomena are verifiable and real."

When in doubt, mimic the prof. "RePEATable," I echoed, taking back the little ships from his hand and depositing them in my pocket. These little bastards were going to move, maybe later than sooner. But move they would!

"Class dismissed," Cosmo said, with a wave of his hand toward the door. "Tom, could you stay for a moment?"

Shit, what have I done or failed to do? Staying after class was a sure recipe for general derision and incessant questions from my classmates.

"So," Cosmo began, once the classroom had cleared. "What's your trick?"

"No trick," I replied, looking him in the eye. "I wish it had worked this time."

"No doubt," he said, slyly. "Honestly, you must have a trick if you were able to fool your classmates. I promise not to tell. If you're a budding magician, I understand that keeping the secret of a trick is important."

"Would it help if I made a video clip of these things actually moving?" I took the bits of paper out of my pocket and let them fall onto the desk again.

"Ha!" Cosmo exploded. "There it is. What a magician can't do live suddenly becomes possible on video. You want to show me a video clip? That's precisely why most magicians find success on television, not in person. So much trickery can be disguised by the camera, especially with video editing software. No, a video would not persuade me. You've heard of George Lucas's company, Industrial Light & Magic? It's called that for a reason."

I didn't know how to respond. Cosmo slung his bookbag over his shoulder and, without another word, walked out of the classroom ahead of me. I stood up from my desk and threw a prolonged, discouraged glance at the scattered bits of paper on the desk.

At that instant, one of the three little ships skittered across the desk and fell onto the floor. "Thanks for nothing," I sputtered half aloud. Cosmo was already far down the hall. I didn't try to call him back.

I guess the James Randi Million Dollar Paranormal Prize would go unclaimed for another day.

Chapter Three
It's a Long Short Story

So. Johnson, my college roommate, who (you will recall) introduced me to Viola, hailed from Minneapolis.

Upon graduation, he joined the family business there—a family events company called FamJam. The firm provides planning and execution for large-scale bar- and bat-mitzvahs, quince años celebrations, anniversaries and assorted private parties. Johnson's first job with FamJam was Post-event Supervisor, a.k.a., cleanup guy.

In late August, he texted me with an offer to work for him. He said that my obsessive tendencies were just what he needed when it came to scooping chicken wings out of swimming pools and condoms off lawns. Lovely work. I think not.

But we stayed in touch during the fall after graduation. Johnson had apparently been looking over my shoulder in our frat house on some of my better 'three ships' moments. More than once, he had witnessed my bits of paper scooting across my desk, unassisted by Industrial Light & Magic. Johnson was mildly amused and downright curious about my abilities.

So was I.

His follow-up text message reached me in early October, four months into my unemployment doldrums: "Yo, bro. My father is friends with a Minneapolis jazz pianist named Erik Vickers. We use him sometimes for our events. Anyway, Vickers is tight with Madame Li—you know, the *Madame Li Magic Show* on TV? If you want five minutes with her, Vickers says he will make it happen. He and she have done music albums together—Madame Li plays jazz flute. So, let me know. You can crash with me and my family. Could be an opportunity to maybe be on TV with that thing you do."

Finding my personal and professional calendar free for the month of October and, for that matter, for the rest of eternity, I called Johnson and asked him to set something up. The idea was to grab a quick moment with Madame Li to demonstrate some homegrown mind-over-matter action. I told Johnson he could come along.

On Tuesday, October 12, I flew into St. Paul International Airport. To my amazement, Johnson was true to his promise to meet my flight.

"You ready to be a star?" he quipped as we zig-zagged through crowds of travelers and out of the airport baggage area.

I laughed. "Yeah, I wouldn't mind a network special of my own. The first five minutes would be earthshaking, but I have no idea what I would do for the rest of the hour. Juggle, I guess."

"You picked up juggling?" Johnson asked.

"No. Would you rather hear me sing?"

Squeezing into the unclaimed space in his FamJam clean-up van, we took the freeway toward his parents' home in the Fulton neighborhood in Minneapolis.

"What do you know about Madame Li?" he asked.

"Quiz me. I'm an encyclopedia."

"OK. So, what's her real name?"

"Easy. Su LI. But she legally changed her name to Madame Li."

"And what's unusual about her?"

"Well, besides the fact that she almost never speaks during her performances, she used to be a U.N. translator. Bizarre, huh?"

"She looks like a translator," Johnson replied. "detail-oriented, picky, right? Good thing she has a backup gig as the most famous female magician in the world."

We turned onto 50th St. "About a mile down there," Johnson pointed to his left, "is the Northview Hotel where Madame Li does a nightly show. That's where you are going to meet her."

I felt a chill of anticipation, indistinguishable from the onset of panic. "When?"

"Tonight," Johnson said, "after her 8 pm show. Vickers, the jazz guy I told you about, got you on Madame Li's schedule for a few minutes."

"So, it's us and the mystery woman." I had read that Madame Li was only 5 feet tall. She was no longer married, but had a college daughter, Lily, with whom she was very close.

Johnson nodded. "Back to the Madame Li quiz. Why does she wear traditional Chinese clothing when she performs?"

I drew a blank. "Tell me, wise one."

"Well, the story changes from time to time, but the most frequent explanation is that she hides a lot of magician's apparatus within her robes."

"Nice. Weird, but nice."

Johnson agreed. "Next question. What is the license plate on her limo?"

"I know this one. Read it in *People* magazine at the dentist's office. 'Presto,' right?"

"Yep. She wants everyone to know she's a magician. Worked very hard to get famous."

"What do you mean?"

"Well," Johnson replied, "look at her hands. Tiny—not particularly good for palming coins and cards."

I didn't really know much about techniques of magic. Johnson scratched his chin, probably to call attention to his effort at a stubble goatee. "Your hands are half again larger than hers. Probably helps you with your magic, true? Did you ever explain how you do the paper thing?"

I shrugged. "Nope. Just something that happens, sometimes. By the way, that's my big worry—that I'll experience a failure to launch in front of Madame Li."

"Can't get it up?" Johnson grinned. "I can stop at a drugstore."

"Xanax would be what I need right now," I said. "But a benzo might throw me off my game."

We pulled into the long driveway of Johnson's family home—an estate, really, with tall white columns and sweeping green lawns.

"Hell," I couldn't help exclaiming. "Shangri-la!"

"Not mine," Johnson said, turning the van into a parking spot to the side of the main house. "My parents' place. Let's get something to eat."

* * * * *

How do you dress to meet Madame Li? I felt that a tie made me look like a missionary. No-one I had seen on our drive was wearing a tie. A few winter coats, though. Temps were already dipping in October. I had brought a sportscoat.

A few hours later, Johnson and I jumped back into the FamJam van for the short drive to the Northview Hotel and my appointment with destiny. I opted for the sportscoat (but not a tie) out of respect for Madame Li.

Erik Vickers, Madame Li's close musician friend, was waiting at the rear stage door of the Northview Theatre when we pulled up.

"Gentlemen," he waved.

I shook hands with Vickers. "Thanks," I said, "for making this introduction. I really appreciate it." My face probably showed my waves of anxiety.

"Of course," he said, reassuringly. "Look, Madame Li is super good about giving a little time to new magicians. Never know when one of them will end up on her TV show."

"From your mouth to God's ear," Johnson stuck in.

Vickers laughed. "You know that's one of her hot buttons. I would stay off the God topic unless you want an earful from her. She doesn't believe in the supernatural."

"No problem," Johnson and I replied, almost in unison.

We walked down a long, narrow hallway carpeted in maroon plush. The Northview Theatre was set off by itself across from a complex of pricey hotel rooms—good thing, I thought, that I could crash at Johnson's place.

"To your right," Vickers directed. "The Green Room."

It wasn't green. The three of us entered a lounge replete with a well-stocked bar, enormous posters of Madame Li on stage, and comfy couches.

"She doesn't drink," Vickers said. "If she offers you something, best to just say no. Fastest way to get on her good side."

Johnson and I nodded together.

"Now," Vickers instructed, "you have a few minutes to get your shit together, so to speak. If you have something to show Madame Li, get it all set up before she gets here. She's very friendly, but she will be looking at her watch the whole time. Don't take it personally. All the plugs are over there." Thinking that I had brought a bevy of tech gear, he motioned toward a bank of electrical outlets.

We made camp in the middle of the lounge. I took a slick-surface cafeteria tray out of my backpack and set it on my knees. The tray looked kind of hokey, but I had no idea in advance where my demonstration would take place. I didn't want to come unprepared.

"That's it?" Vickers chuckled. "You should see the technology some guys unload for their show-and-tell with Madame Li."

"I brought just the minimum," I responded. "The basics, right?"

"Wise," Vickers confirmed. "Madame Li has seen it all in terms of hi-tech for magic. You're smart to keep it simple. That's what she likes best."

At that moment, the door to the Green Room opened and the Mystery Woman swept in. She was still dressed in her elaborate Chinese gown for the stage. Johnson and I leapt to our feet. My cafeteria tray flipped off my knees and clattered to the floor.

"Madame Li," Vickers said, "meet your next great act— Tom the Magician. And I think you know Johnson here. He's the FamJam guy who cleaned up after the event at your house last month."

Madame Li flashed her gracious, welcoming smile. "Fantastic. Welcome to Minneapolis, Tom!" She sank into a chair across from us and exhaled. "Sit down, sit down. God, I am getting too old for these shows every night. Still exciting, but—whew!" Grinning, she blew a long, relaxed whistle of air.

I fumbled for something appropriate to say. Vickers gave me a little cover by excusing himself: "I've gotta get back to making music," he said, looking first at Madame Li, then at us. "Tom, I will leave you in the capable hands of The Ultimate Magician." With that, Vickers gave a playful salute to Madame Li and made a quick exit.

I had regained my bearings a bit. "I must admit I'm nervous, Madame Li." Better to get it out there.

"Nerves," she laughed. "I feel butterflies before every performance."

I reached for my cafeteria tray and set it on my knees again. "I know you're very busy. I really appreciate just a couple minutes of your time."

"No problem," she smiled, focusing intently on my cafeteria tray. "So, that's your prop?"

I returned her smile and began to relax. "Yeah, this is the starter's kit. Came with a book of instructions."

Madame LI apparently liked my attempt at humor. "The last guy had a whole bank of computers against that wall," she said, pointing. "I'm still paying the electric bill."

"No electricity here," I replied, flipping the tray over once to show that I had no hidden apparatus.

"OK, let the act begin," she invited, looking at her watch for the first time. "Actually, before you begin, just take a minute to talk me through things. What am I going to see? You don't have to tell me how it works."

I started to respond, but caught myself. "Madame Li, let me be completely honest. I am not a magician, as far as I know. I've never really performed in my life. What I will show you is nothing very impressive. Kick me out as soon as you get bored."

I took a sheet of ordinary typing paper out of my pocket and quickly tore off three postage-sized bits. "The basic idea is that I will make these little pieces of paper—" I folded them quickly into my familiar ships—"travel across this tray for a foot or so. I swear it's not an act."

"The exact words of some of the biggest names in magic," she said, with a serious glint in her eyes. "They want people to believe that they truly have supernatural powers, not magicians' skills. You don't believe you have superhuman abilities, do you?"

Her steely tone told me that I had better answer "no." Madame Li apparently had a special place in hell designated for magicians who claimed supernatural powers.

"No, I'm not claiming anything. I'm just stuck with this kinda stupid routine that I can't understand. Let me show you and get your advice."

"Ha! That's a fabulous intro," Madame Li beamed. "The ingénue who has no clue about what he's really doing. I love it."

I frowned a little in confusion. "Honest to God, I don't know how this works."

"OK, OK." She leaned back in her chair. "But before you begin, let me look at your two props—the tray and the paper bits."

I handed them to her.

She held the tray up to the light and examined it carefully, then did the same thing with the bits of paper.

"Looks like—" she paused for effect—"an ordinary cafeteria tray. Am I right or wrong?"

"You're right. A tray stolen from the cafeteria at Boston College."

"And the paper?"

"Torn from this sheet of typing paper," I answered, handing her remainder of the sheet. I noticed that her fast, small hands swirled quickly around mine for an instant, as if checking for hidden threads or God knows what.

"So, this is all of it?" she questioned, getting serious now about the possible misdirection and deceptions that might be at play. "Woud you mind taking off your sportscoat and rolling up your sleeves? Tell me if this will throw you off your game. I'm just trying to cut to the chase." She glanced at her watch again.

"No game," I said, "at least not one that I'm aware of." I took off my sportscoat and rolled up my sleeves to my elbows. She handed me back my tray and paper bits.

Without fanfare, I set the tray on my knees again and placed my three little ships at one edge of the tray. "Now," I said, "if it works, you will see—" I squeezed my mind into concentration on the bits of paper—"these little paper ships move across—" I squeezed again—"the perilous seas of this tray." I stuck in the 'perilous seas' thing at the last second. After all, I was in the presence of Madame Li. "In the building," as they said of Elvis.

And, to my eternal relief, the bits of paper started to move, an inch or so at first before stopping, with one moving ahead of another as if in a race. I wrinkled my face in concentration—what Johnson called my constipation expression—and tried to coax my ships all the way across the tray. Within about 20 seconds they had made the transit and arrived safely at the distant shore.

Madame Li leaned forward. "Let me see the tray again." I handed it to her. She tapped it in several places. "And now the paper, please."

One by one, she unfolded the little paper ships, actually smelling each and touching one to her tongue. "I'm not asking you to tell me your technique. Magicians don't do that, except maybe after too many drinks at the Magic Castle in Hollywood. But give me a hint. Are you somehow blowing air on these things? It's not magnetism, as far as I can tell, and I would have spotted threads by now. Some kind of static electrical effect?"

"Madame Li," I started, realizing that she was deeply engaged in what she had seen, "if I could explain this, I would. It doesn't work most of the time. In fact, I'm relieved that it worked tonight."

"Hmm," she murmured, her hand touching her cheek. "Wait just a minute." She opened the door and called "Benson!" down the hallway. In a moment, we were joined by her assistant, a large, middle-aged man who introduced himself as Troy Benson—"call me Troy." He wore a tailored gray suit and magenta tie. I shook his hand.

"Benson," Madame Li said, motioning him to a chair, "this is Tom, who doesn't know if he's a magician or not. He's doing something here you should see. Do you want to see those bits of paper move across the tray?" With that intro, I set the tray on my knees again, prepared with bated breath for another demonstration—or failure.

Benson waved his hands. "Wait!" He reached over and took the tray, setting it down beside him with obvious care. He placed his hands together, palms up, forming his own preferred surface for my display. With a coy smile, he motioned for me to make my little paper ships move across his upturned hands.

"How rude," Madame Li shamed him in fun. "You are the devil, Benson. This is exactly why young people give up on careers in magic. Let the kid use his tray! It's part of his act."

"No," I interrupted, "let's do it his way. Who knows?" I placed each of my paper ships next to Benson's thumb on his left palm. "Maybe these bits of paper—" I started to knit my eyebrows in concentration—"will . . . travel . . . across to his right palm."

Thank you, Jesus, Mary, and Joseph. All the saints, too. The paper bits were moving, none too quickly, each ship in jerks making its way across Benson's hands. The ships plinked noiselessly off his right palm onto the floor. Benson gave a questioning look to Madame Li, who shrugged a silent "hell-if-I-know" response.

"OK, try it again on my playing field." Madame Li adjusted herself in her chair and stuck out her own palms, much smaller than Benson's. "You made it across the ocean," she joked. "See what you can do with this little lake."

I set my ships at the edge of one of Madame Li's palms and bore down in mental effort. The bits were still cooperating. In uneven motion, they moved one ahead of another until all had reached the edge of her other palm. She squeezed her fist shut, keeping the little ships from falling to the floor.

Without a segue, Madame Li began whispering to Benson in the shorthand language of consummately skilled magicians. Benson, I gathered, was no slouch when it came to the craft of magic. I understood none of what they were saying. Occasionally a name would pop out— Randi, Swami Rama, Houdini, and many I had never heard of. This intense dialogue went on for perhaps a full five minutes, conducted between the two as if Johnson and I were not in the room. They apparently reached a conclusion of some kind, then both looked up at me.

"Tom," Madame Li began, her hands waving as if to re-set a table. "This is cool. This is very cool." She paused, deciding how to continue. "Simple, elegant, mysterious. As I said earlier, the art of the ingénue. To tell you the truth, I have seen nothing exactly like it—certainly nothing that took place on my own hands." Benson looked at his own hands and vigorously shook his head in agreement.

"I'm glad you liked it," I blurted out. I wanted to ask them precisely what they wanted to ask me: *how does this work?*

"Let's kill the elephant in the room," Madame Li said in a patient, quiet tone. "Tom, we have to assume that you don't have actual superhuman abilities, do you agree?"

"I have no idea," I replied. "It started when I was fifteen. And with just bits of paper so far. I've tried it with pennies, marbles, ball bearings, dominoes, beer caps, you name it. No luck at all. And if I get more than a few feet from the bits of paper, I can't make it happen, no matter how hard I concentrate."

Madame Li and Benson appeared to be taking close mental notes. She picked up the thread of discussion. "And you say you can't make this trick, act, whatever, happen on command? Sometimes it misfires?"

"Exactly. Most of the time, in fact," I answered. "I'm glad it worked tonight." Johnson patted me on the shoulder, as if to say 'way to go.'

Benson's eyes were dark with intense interest. He whispered something in Madame Li's ear.

She smiled at me. "Benson said, not ready for prime time." "Your trick is fabulous, but what would you do on stage or on camera? I mean, imagine that we put you on my TV show. If your act goes south that night—you said it only worked sometimes—we all look, well, silly. And that would be a shame. You pull off the 'Duh, I-don't-know' thing really well. Without revealing anything you don't want to share, you are aware of how you do this, right?"

Madame Li had asked a serious question and expected absolute honesty from me.

"I swear, there's nothing I'm not telling you." I felt my cheeks growing hot. But my nose wasn't growing.

"People are funny," Madame Li mused. "You can tell them they are going to see a spoon continue to bend even when it is set by itself on a table. You take out a previously bent spoon and begin twirling it on the tabletop before their eyes. By and large, they will swear that they are watching the spoon bend even more. That's the power of suggestion. You pick up the spoon, give it a hidden last bend between your thumb and fingers for good measure, and present it to them. Ta-da! Gasps of disbelief—really, gasps of belief. Seeing what we believe—one of our strangest and weakest traits as human beings."

Another behind-the-hand whisper to Madame Li from Benson.

"And," Madame Li finished, "maybe that's what's happening here. Benson and I may be under your spell somehow. Suggestion, hypnotism, all that Mesmer stuff. Damn good if you pulled that off with us. Doing your act on our own hands was genius."

Madame Li and Benson stood up, offered congratulations all around, and jotted down my contact information. They were obviously intrigued, maybe even baffled by what they had seen. As was I.

I found myself wishing there was, in fact, some hi-tech or sneaky mental trick at work here. Johnson and I thanked Madame Li profusely for her time and interest.

Benson walked us back down the long hallway toward our van. "We'll be in touch," he said, shaking my hand earnestly. "I don't know exactly how or when, but we will be in touch."

I wilted into the passenger seat of the FamJam van as Johnson steered out of the Theatre's parking lot. I was exhausted. The evening had gone well. I hadn't made a fool of myself. My ships hadn't sunk on this, their most important harbor tour.

I didn't realize I had lit a fuse.

Chapter Four
True Believers

Back to college for a bit, at least in memory. It's toward the end of my freshman year. True stories here. Couldn't make them up.

Johnson, it turns out, had loose lips. He told assorted classmates about my start-and-stop forays into psychokinesis. And he had backup: Viola was also talking, not so much about my prowess as a lover (alas) as my occasional success as Mental Master of the Paper Bits.

"Tom, you're rushing Alpha Phi?" Midway through my freshman year, an intimidating senior (let's call him Ishmael, what the heck) stepped into my dorm room without knocking. The big cheese of my target fraternity stoops to conquer.

"Uh, yeah," I stumbled. Was this bad news already? I hadn't even completed the interviews with my would-be frat brothers.

"Here's my advice," he began, sitting on the edge of my neatly-made bed. Asperger's never sleeps, especially in an unmade bed. He motioned me toward my desk chair. "Figure out something you have to offer the fraternity."

"Such as?" If he could cut to the chase, so could I.

"Well, you're not an athlete or a National Merit Scholar, right?"

"That would be correct."

"No particular musical ability or artistic flair?"

"Nope." I hoped this was leading somewhere.

"Not exactly a people person, either?"

I shrugged. "You might say."

"Tom, you have to get your shit together and tell the brothers what you bring to the table. The frat is not a social charity. Every brother has something special. So, what separates you from all the schmucks who aren't going to get in?"

Nothing particular came to mind. I looked down.

"For God's sake," he continued, "look at this place. Your shoes are all lined up in the closet. Your books are in alphabetical order on the shelf. Who makes their bed in college? Shit, man. You're not exactly frat material. We need to come up with something right now, right here."

Would he be here if I really didn't have a chance? I thought not. "I'm not your average candidate, that's true," I said, finding my voice. "I guess I do magic, in a way. That would be something new for the frat, correct?"

"Might be," he replied, "although last year we had one guy who did card tricks. He failed out."

A beat of silence fell. "I don't really do tricks," I offered. "It's more like mental powers . . . making things move, that sort of thing."

"Yeah," he responded, "Johnson told me. Wads of paper, right?"

"Well, not exactly wads. I fold them like this." I reached for an ever-present swatch of paper on my desk.

"I don't want to see you fold fucking wads of paper," he muttered. "You do magic tricks, correct?"

I put the paper down. "I don't know if I would call it magic. I can make little stuff move with my mind. Sometimes."

"What do you mean, sometimes?"

"I mean that I can't control when it works. But I can do it. Johnson has seen it. What did he tell you?"

"All he said was that you had something unique to show to the brothers, something we can roll out at parties or whatever. True?"

"True and false. Like I said, I can't make it work on demand. Not the kind of thing you would headline for an Alpha Phi party."

"That is becoming pretty damn obvious," he shot back, standing. "Well, do your best in the interviews. Who knows?" He shook his head and walked out. Asshole.

Veni, vidi, vici. I came to the interviews, I saw, and I succeeded, maybe by just a hair. I'm a card-carrying Alpha Phi brother. I haven't been asked to perform at any parties.

But, thanks to Johnson and Viola, word got out in the frat house that, as one brother put it, "Tom is up to some really weird shit." In dribs and drabs, believers began finding their way to my door.

Turns out my frat had more than its share of the curious and desperate. To wit:

"Tom, will you do your mental thing online to change a couple grades for me? If you can move paper, you can certainly flip a couple bits and bytes in the mainframe. Com'on, man!"

"Tom, stare at my knee for a few minutes. I wrenched something. Make it fast, though. I've got a game this afternoon."

"Tom, this is a picture of Linda. Just put your hex on it so I have a chance with her this weekend. I heard you do voodoo."

"Tom, you've got to help me. I can't find my phone."

No healing, no voodoo, no cyber-crime, certainly no phone location service. But, as a compliant freshman, I always gave the requests of my frat brothers the old college try. After all, I was still experimenting with my powers, such as they were.

In one case, the guy said his knee felt a little better. In another, my mystical revelation that the brother's phone was somewhere in his room proved miraculously accurate. Of course, I was an abject failure in delivering most of the time. My potential reputation as the resident witch doctor quickly flickered out. In truth, I was relieved.

One cling-on parent, however, proved to be a true believer with staying power. Meet the memorable mother of a frat brother, Robert. He was a bit obsessed, it turns out, with mentalism in all its forms. He told his mother all about me, no doubt inflating each detail. She called me with an invitation.

"Tom, my son Robert has told me about your abilities." (My experiments had turned into 'abilities,' at least in her mind. Progress!) "We have a spiritual interest group meeting not far from the university once a month. Would you be available as our guest for lunch?"

The attention felt good. I gladly accepted her invitation and, hey, it's free food.

On a Thursday late in the spring semester, the reality of the 'spiritual' meeting turned out to be a poke in the eye with a sharp stick. A group of 60-somethings, long on the 'somethings,' gathered around a luncheon table at the Alpine Smorgasbord a short walk from campus. They had a place for me at the head of the table. Robert's mother, the obvious mover and pusher for the group, introduced me.

"And here, friends, is Tom, our guest for this month's meeting and a fraternity brother of my son, Robert. Tom is interested in the powers of the mind and spirit, as we all are. He's here to share his experiences with us. Maybe even a demonstration, Tom?" She smiled. I groaned inside. I think the frat expression is "threw up in my mouth." You get the idea.

Asperger's doesn't put you at the head of the class in public speaking. I struggled to cough up an off-the-cuff talk of sorts about my psychokinetic ability. I could tell from the slack, dull faces of the old geezers before me that either I was mumbling or they were half deaf. My story about moving paper bits didn't seem to interest them.

To my surprise when it came time for questions, all hell broke loose—literally.

"Tom, did you have a religious upbringing? Has anyone educated you about the work of Satan?" (Uh, no and no.)

"Does God speak to you when you go into your trance?" (What trance? For that matter, what god?)

"Do you accept Jesus Christ as your personal savior?" (That's a big bite away from bits of paper.)

"Have you laid your hands upon a sick person? What was the result?" (I guess I have inadvertently touched at least one sick person in my life to date, but not with the idea of healing them. Just wanted them to move so I could get off the subway.)

Lunch rescued me from the appetites of these true believers. Picture the rubber chicken and faux mashed potatoes. And then, mercifully, it was over. Robert's mom walked me to the restaurant exit.

"Tom, thanks so, so much for joining our group today." (Joining them? I was now a member? Yikes.) "We will all pray for you. Psychic abilities can be a gift from God or the work of the devil."

She had touched a nerve. I asked her, "And how do you tell the difference?"

Her eyes flickered instinctively toward heaven and grew a little misty. "Faith speaks to faith, Tom. In our group, we all sense when we are in the presence of the Spirit. God wants to live in each of us, including you. But the devil walketh about as a roaring lion, seeking whom he may devour." Robert's mother suddenly spouteth Renaissance English, forsooth. "Tom, do you smell sulfur when you attempt your supernatural feats?"

We now stood outside the restaurant. I sniffed the air involuntarily. In truth, there was a whiff of sulfur about— perhaps just her perfume.

"No," I responded. "Sometimes a nutmeg smell or allspice, but never sulfur." I couldn't help myself.

She smiled benevolently. "Well, that's a good sign. I can't tell you to keep up the good work, since it hasn't been shown to be good. But we will pray for you. Did I mention that?"

Uh-huh.

My walk back to the frat house gave me time to reflect. How in the hell (cancel that, wrong reference) did my paper-pushing abilities morph into connections with

Satan's work (everyone needs a job), the Blood of the
Lamb (best served rare), and the eternal welfare of *moi*?
I really had never considered the ultimate sources of my
mental powers. Satan? Hadn't met the guy, but would
look more closely at lions in the future. My personal Lord
and Savior, Jesus Christ? Hadn't met him, either, but
reminder to self: Search the Bible for miracles involving
bits of paper.

Game on if the Son of God wanted to go head to head with
me in the miraculous acts department, and this time
without the stench of loaves and fishes. Ditto for water
into wine, one of the oldest tricks in any magician's bag of
tricks, if you can overlook bad wine.

Why had this group chosen me for their special interest
and spiritual investigation? In a small way I represented,
at least once in a while, what they were waiting for—an
authentic confrontation with the supernatural. They were
all waiting for a miracle, and none too patiently. I was
their canary in the mineshaft, chirping out the possibility
that God was alive and active in the world. Some of them
had probably spent their lives begging God (operating
through Jesus, the Holy Spirit, the Saints, Mary, Our Lady
of Lourdes, the Shroud of Turin—hard to choose a port of
entry) to relieve their bunions, reduce their rent,
straighten out their wayward children, whatever.

Had their prayers been answered? Hard to say. Maybe
this college kid, Tom, was God's quirky way of being more

obvious in the world. Robert's mom and her friends were mulling the possibility that I, God's paper-moving servant on Earth, hid breaking news from Upstairs.

To true believers, I might be a tiny, smoldering ember from the divine fire. Like Mark Twain and Nikola Tesla before them, these were men and women captivated by a séance of sort. They searched earnestly for some sign of God in their existence. Frankly, I had never thought of my bits of paper as God-among-us. I would have to give them (the bits) more respect in the future.

Johnson was out—I hoped not with Viola—when I returned to the frat house by mid-afternoon. I felt unusually tired (fleeing from the lion, after all) and flopped down on my well-made bed. The phrase "seeking whom he may devour" kept running through my mind. Verbal obsession is right near the top of Asperger's symptoms. Was my flirtation with psychic powers laced somehow with the devil's brew or prodded by the Rod of Jesse?

Hell, no. Heavens, no. Take your pick.

I yawned before drifting into a nap. I may be insane, but I'm not crazy.

Chapter Five
Don Quixote Advises Me

Millennials like me—those who don't know what a telephone operator or *TV Guide* (the magazine) is—are equally ignorant of past psychic players like Don Quixote, a 1980s sensation. Don Quixote, of course, was his stage name. He was born Emil Rodriguez Cretin. The Quixote moniker, he explained in one press interview, was his nod to all who tilted at windmills in whatever form.

His name came up at my luncheon with Robert's mom and her spiritual stormtroopers. ("Tom, you remind us of Don Quixote, that Satanist mindreader from Mexico." I sensed that Mexico wasn't high on their list of divine destinations, a few shrines not withstanding. And mindreading had to be just plain perverse for their generation. Who would peak behind the mask?)

I googled "Don Quixote, Magician" in search of a soulmate and possible mentor in my increasingly confusing world of psychic endeavor. I learned that he had a worldwide following in the 1980s and beyond, to the point of spontaneous neighborhood mindreading clubs throughout the world. The neighbors would gather, pair off, and attempt the "Think of a number" routine made famous by Quixote. Any success in guessing the correct number (being close counted for many neighbors) brought howls of amazement from the group, and local fame for the winners.

Don Quixote's special talent was selecting a random audience member (if you believe that) and transmitting his or her thoughts to Quixote's assistant sitting blindfolded on stage. To a rush of OMG's from the audience, a seemingly miraculous stream of items appeared to be mentally broadcast from Quixote to his confederate—the exact contents of a wallet or purse, middle name of a grandparent, last two numbers of a Social Security number, and so forth. The most amazed person in the hall, of course, appeared to be the person whose mind was being read.

In his performances, Quixote was maddeningly silent on the question of trick or treat, the latter connoting supernatural power. "Watch and I will let you judge for yourself," he typically proclaimed. Decent of him. "Don't be skeptical. Open your mind. Believe and be positive!" Ah, the power of belief in human affairs! Preparing the mindset of one's target audience is half the battle in influencing perception.

An M.I.T. professor decided to put Quixote to the test on September 4, 1982. The TV audience was huge for the event. The professor challenged Quixote to perform his mindreading act by correctly sending four single-digit numbers, in order, to his confederate—located, by the professor's requirement, in another room at the University.

The result, no doubt to Quixote's regret, was cerebral dysfunction of the first order. Unable to make anything happen, Quixote protested to the professor that "scientific static in the building" was preventing his mind messages from getting through to his assistant. His confederate said that only one digit came through clearly from Quixote. But, alas, that transmission was not one of the four digits selected for the experiment.

Quixote's widely-publicized failure ("Mind Goes Numb," a national newspaper reported) was a devastating strike against his reputation for millions of viewers. Apparently, the American audience gave any Man Who Would Be Shaman only one bite at the apple.

I, however, give Quixote credit. As with my hit-and-miss moments with bits of paper, he couldn't get it up on command when it came to beaming his thoughts through walls. Classic performance anxiety, no doubt. Or the vagaries of a "spirit," be it Satanic or angelic? Who knows, who cares. He failed miserably at M.I.T., and, shortly thereafter, took his show to Mexico and a new audience. He resides there to this day.

This 'career pivot,' as we say, was good for me even if it wasn't for Quixote. Since he was no longer in avid public demand (he now sells and teaches a seminar on mindreading for amateur magicians), he might actually respond to email contact from an aspiring supernaturalist, if that's what I was.

Halfway through my sophomore year, I located Quixote's email and wrote to him.

"Mr. Quixote, I'm a fan who has seen on video your many amazing displays of mental powers. I am assuming you still have these abilities. They don't go away, do they? I ask this because I find myself with the ability to move small bits of paper across a tabletop with my mind. I can send you a video clip of this phenomenon. Hoping that we can connect on our shared interests and experiences. Yours sincerely."

The last phrase apparently sounded too much like a business letter. I received an automated business reply.

"Thank you for your interest in future appearances by Don Quixote. Although his performance calendar is quite full for the foreseeable future, he welcomes bookings for large and small occasions. His fee schedule is available upon request."

Maybe someday I will have a fee schedule, I day-dreamed. Galileo's last words were supposedly "E pur si muove" ("And yet it moves!"), referring to his obviously Satanic idea that the Earth revolves around the Sun. He must have been lionized in his day, so to speak. I made a mental note to use Galileo's words, "Yet it moves!", in advertising my first appearance on one of the late-night Jimmys—Kimmel or Fallon.

But for the nonce, I had to get in direct contact with Don Quixote, not his booking service. I tried another, more succinct email message.

"Mr. Quixote, I desperately need to contact you. I am struggling with a mysterious power to move things with my mind alone. I am neither a kook nor a camp follower. In fact, I am a member of the Alpha Phi fraternity. I am in good standing, as far as I know, as a student at a bonafide American university. Please contact me."

To receive disclosing communication from others, you yourself have to disclose. I think that's a corollary of the Golden Rule. I attached a one-minute video showing me herding my bits and pieces sans hands or tricks.

I knew from press records that Quixote made it habit to reach into a bin of printed email messages to fetch those that mattered most, as guided by the spirits. My message made the cut. Don responded a few days later.

"Gracias, Tom. I am appearing at a supper club, the Silver Slipper, in New York City on March 18 at 8 pm, for one show only. If you buy a ticket for that show, I will be happy to meet with you after the performance for a few minutes. Although I receive many requests for help from aspiring mentalists and psychics, I am intrigued by your video. Quite convincing! Peace and blessing. Don Q."

Not everyone receives Don's blessing, I guessed. I hoped it didn't somehow zap the continued prayers I was still receiving from Robert's mom and her group. I scrabbled together the $48 required for a ticket to Quixote's NYC appearance on March 18.

The show itself was, shall we say, "intimate." About 50 people huddled over cocktails in dim light. Most were transitioning from gray to white in the hair department. Ever the consummate showman, Quixote gave them their money's worth. His 90-minute act was replete with disclosing details about his life ("My first memory as a child was reading my mother's mind," "I was struck by lightning, which amplified my mind powers"), advice on at-home mindreading ("Concentrate all your abilities on one word—'READ"), and nicely performed illusions and other marvels. I say 'illusions' with the assumption that Don was a skilled magician, not someone possessed of superhuman abilities. I hoped that he did not make the same assumption about me.

At the end of the show, Don dashed offstage after a couple curtain calls. 'Offstage' is my euphemism for 'behind a screen.' The Silver Slipper didn't have an offstage or green room. As the mini-crowd moved to the exit, I bucked the trend and stepped forward to find Don.

"Mr. Quixote," I called, thinking he had forgotten our after-show appointment. I was right.

He looked out from the screen, focusing on me and wrinkling his brow. His eyes were dark. I could see why he had such a riveting presence on stage.

"Call me Don, please. An autograph?" he asked.

"No. I'm Tom from Boston College. You said we could meet for a few minutes after tonight's show. It was great, by the way."

He covered his forgetfulness well. "Of course—Tom. Let's sit down." He motioned toward one of the front tables.

We sat. I noticed how drained he looked up close after the evening performance. His 70-plus years were showing.

"You are a magician, correct?" he queried, trying to move things along and still not recalling why I was here.

"Yes and no," I replied. "I'm stuck with what some people call a trick. Making pieces of paper move with my mind."

"Uh-huh," he nodded, not fully in the moment. "I'm familiar with the routine." How many wannabes had come to him for advice?

I pressed on. "I don't think it's a trick. At least, I'm not aware that I'm doing anything."

Expecting him to ask for a demonstration, I paused. He didn't ask.

"Tom," he said, leaning toward me, "all illusions depend on an audience's need to believe. The longer you can keep them guessing about 'is it real or an illusion?', the greater your power over them. Do you remember the TV ad—"Is it real or is it Memorex?" No, you're too young. But you're on the right track playing dumb about what you do. People don't want to be tricked by magic. They want to believe in magic. 'When you wish upon a star . . . .' All that Disney stuff is based on our deep need to believe."

I smiled and felt myself relaxing a bit. "Dumb is the right word. I'm deaf, dumb, and blind to what's really going on. Really." I pushed hard on the last word.

"Great," he said, smiling back. "Just great. Feigned naivete is the best ticket to success. Everyone is looking for an authentic guru, not another trickster no matter how skilled. You're playing your hand just right." He pushed back his chair to signal that our conversation was ending.

But, hey, I had paid $48 for this moment with Don. That should buy at least another question. "Why," I blurted out, "can't I get my paper bits to move every time on command? I fail nine times out of ten. That's friggin' embarrassing."

He laughed. "So true." Maybe he was recalling his performance failure at M.I.T. decades ago. "The answer is, control your environment," he offered, still wrapping things up with me. "Figure out ways to gain complete control of that environment—someone on the inside, someone on the outside, someone your audience would never suspect. Then your illusions will succeed every time."

"But," I began, "I don't think my—" He cut me off with a wave of his hand.

"You're the genuine article, right?" he laughed again, without sarcasm. "The real deal. Keep that up. Everyone wants to believe there's someone on Earth with supernatural powers. Jesus. Buddha. The Wizard of Oz. They all played it dumb and the world beat a path to their door."

He reached into his breast pocket and pulled out a playing card bearing his name. "A souvenir." He handed it to me with a little professional flourish. "And good luck. Stay dumb as long as possible!" This time he vanished not behind the stage screen but out the front door to a waiting car. I noticed it wasn't a limo.

On the train back to Boston that night I gathered my thoughts about Don Quixote, his illusions, and whatever in the hell I was experiencing with mind over matter. His phrase echoed: "they want to believe." So, was this all some kind of mass hypnosis, a spell that had grabbed not only my audiences but me as well? Was I believing so hard that I distorted what I was seeing, what was real? And what's with my performance failures? Was I failing to believe hard enough?

I shook off the thought. There's no way I had fallen down some rabbithole into Blunderland. After all, I was the chief skeptic of my so-called supernatural powers. I just wanted to understand them.

Chapter Six
Brain Waves

It's now the first semester of my senior year at Boston College. Time flies.

I realized this week that I had never used my university health insurance or the student health center in my time here. I—or my parents, more accurately—have paid $2000 or more in university healthcare premiums up to this point. Although I am not ill, I felt I should use this untapped resource, if only to fill some gaps in my understanding of psychokinesis.

Specifically, I aimed to visit (ok, obsessed on visiting) the university health center to check out a possible explanation for my power over paper bits--not much of a supernatural empire, I admit. I had a strong suspicion that my mind was broadcasting a beam of energy somehow. In my late-night reveries, I pictured my brain sending out a Trek-like tractor beam to draw the paper bits toward me.

But how to prove it? I knew that the brain uses twenty percent of the body's total energy, based on a 2400 calorie diet. Gram for gram of tissue, the brain consumes ten times the amount of energy compared to the rest of the body. Given the total electrical output of about 100 watts for the entire body, that means 20 watts or so are buzzing around my brain, and maybe beyond my brain to my paper bits.

"May I help you?" The receptionist was obviously a student worker, probably an underclassman. She stood ready to put a clipboard in my hand with a sheaf-load of medical forms to fill out and sign.

"Sure," I replied. "I would like to get an EEG." We stared at each other for a moment.

"Do you mean an EKG?" she asked, holding back a yawn. Definitely a student worker.

"No, EEG," I clarified, tapping my temple to give her a clue. "You know, brain waves. I need to be checked for a brain beam."

She appeared to be jotting down 'brain beam' followed by several question marks. "Are you ill?" she asked.

"I don't know. That's why I'm here," I tried to explain. "And I haven't used any of my health benefits in my three-plus years at the university. I'm due."

She told me to take a seat. I didn't sense that I was on the Urgent list, as far as she was concerned.

A couple hours later, a forty-something nurse called me to the inner sanctum. Another Green Room of sorts. "What are you here for?" she asked. "Brain beam. What is that?"

I tried to translate. "I think I have energy flowing out of my brain toward, well, stuff outside. Maybe 'beam' isn't the right word. I think I need an EEG," I answered.

She patronized me. "Do you know what an EEG is?"

"Electroencephalogram," I shot back. I didn't appreciate her deprecating tone. I was a college senior, after all.

"What are your symptoms?" Her eyes narrowed, not unlike a tractor beam. Maybe I had come to the right place.

"I think my brain is sending out an energy beam of some kind. I can move little bits of paper with my mind."

She gave me a quizzical look. "I . . . see. Do you have seizures or intense headaches? Have you visited a psychologist or psychiatrist in the last, say, ten years?"

I didn't know where this was going. "No, I'm perfectly well. I just need a quick EEG to check out my brain waves."

"A quick EEG," she echoed.

"Yes," I answered, thinking she was coming on board. "My theta and delta waves are probably OK, but I suspect that either my alpha or beta waves are much stronger than usual."

She raised her stylus from the tablet in her hand. "The doctor . . . well, just sit down. She will be here in a few minutes." The nurse had gone glassy-eyed. Perhaps my brain waves were affecting her. I can't control my tractor beam.

The doctor popped in a couple moments later. She had the brusque air of someone behind in their appointments and eager to move along. I figured I had 60 seconds at best to tell her what I wanted. Scratch that: what I *needed.*

I politely requested an EEG. The doctor looked at her watch, then at me. "It's highly unlikely that your brain is beaming out anything," she said, fighting back a smile. "Alpha and beta waves can be measured," she continued, "but they are very, very weak. You say you move things with your mind?"

I briefly summed up my paper-bit resume, dropping in the name of Madame Li. She didn't seem impressed. Maybe she had watched Don Quixote on the M.I.T. telecast.in 1982.

"Are you under psychiatric care?" she asked. I was nonplussed. Did she think I was crazy?

"Absolutely not," I answered.

"Well," she said, writing as she spoke, "we have no EEG in this facility. And, lacking symptoms, you won't qualify for a brain workup of any kind. I can make an appointment for you with a mental health counsellor."

This was going nowhere fast. "I just wanted to sign up for an EEG," I replied. "It's my alpha waves, I think. Too strong, maybe."

"Alpha waves," the doctor repeated, her words damp with impatience verging on loathing. "The next available appointment with a mental health counsellor is next Monday at 2 pm. Would that work for you?"

I declined. I was interested in waves, not counseling. In fact, the only stress I felt was frustration at not getting an EEG, especially since the university had taken payment for my unused health insurance for the past three years. I did finally get an EEG some years later, with—as the university doctor predicted—no significant result. And it was at my own expense, I may add. So much for health premiums.

My alpha, beta, theta and delta waves were not remarkable in any way. If I did broadcast a beam from my brain, it evidenced itself whimsically and inconsistently, and certainly not in the doctor's office. Sounds familiar.

But the brain wave theory had been worth exploring. Although the brain operates on decent wattage, not so for its amperage—very low, hardly measurable. And, of course, there's no practical way of connecting to the brain's electrochemical circuitry. Even if I could plug a cord into my head, it would take about 285 days to charge an iPhone battery, with its capacity of 5.4 watt hours. There's the additional glitch that drawing off the brain's electrical energy means sacrificing a few things, like breathing and a heartbeat.

At one point, I thought the sheer size of my brain might explain my paper play. Like Coleridge, I sometimes felt that my brain was going to explode out of my skull. My head, as my roommate mentioned more than once, was large. But then, so was Einstein's. His brain, however, was about 15 percent smaller than that of a typical adult male. I had little luck persuading the university health center to measure the size of my brain, my paid-up health premiums not withstanding.

Perhaps I would donate my brain to science, as did Einstein. My heirs would find out if size really mattered. And what university health center doesn't have an EEG machine or brain measurement services for prepaid customers?

Chapter Seven
Voila, Viola!

You recall Viola. Our initial tryst, facilitated by Johnson, demonstrated to Vi and me that we still had training wheels on when it came to a moveable feast of sexual connection. Not that it was a failure. Sex was OK--in fact, very OK. We just found ourselves giggling a lot, often at inopportune moments. We are now equal parts friends and lovers.

In that context, we meet once a week or so at the Dive to unburden ourselves of life's many annoyances and conundrums. Here's an approximate transcript from last night's conversation.

Me: I want to apologize.

Her: For what?

Me: My obsession with moving things. It has gotten really sick.

Her: Sick how?

Me: I think about it way too much and talk about it too often. You must be bored out of your mind.

Her: You're wrong. I'm interested. I mean, not everyone can move things with their mind.

Me: Not anyone except me. See, there I go again.

Her: So, why does it matter so much to you?

Me: The ability to move things?

Her: Yeah. Why is it so important?

Me: I've told you about my lean-in toward Asperger's. There's no answer to why—I just nit-pick certain things to death.

Her: Like what?

Me: Depends. I focus on schedules, making sure I'm exactly on time for appointments, a particular TV show, or getting up at precisely the same time each morning. I went through a stage as a food freak—have to eat this, won't ever eat that. I knew one Asperger's kid in high school who had to wear a specific color for each day of the week. Monday was blue, Tuesday was red, Wednesday was yellow, that sort of thing. Never varied the entire year. Her mother tried to break the pattern, but that only led to tears and family arguments.

Her: Bizarre. So, your obsession now is moving paper? You can't just turn it off?

Me: Nope. I obsess, and then I obsess on obsessing. It just feels right. Let's say, for argument's sake, that I try to avoid any thought of my mental abilities. It's like trying not to think of a banana split. You end up hungrier than before.

Her: God, a banana split sounds fabulous. Do they have them here?

Me: See, that makes my point. Resisting an obsession just ends up feeding it.

Her: I read a line from William Blake in my lit class yesterday. "Throw him in the lake who loves water."

Me: Meaning?

Her: The prof said it meant that we should give in to our impulses and desires, not ignore or resist them.

Me: When I'm with you, I don't think so much about moving bits of paper. You are the antidote to obsession.

Her: That's sweet. I haven't been called an antidote.

Me: I guess it's something like this. You have seen me do my thing with paper. I don't have to prove anything to you.

Her: Not at all.

Me: But with most other people I meet, I feel like I'm a big nothing until I reveal my secret skills. If there's the slightest opportunity, I've got to tell them. Maybe show them.

Her: Must be like Clark Kent—you know, hiding his Superman identity but, inside, dying to get out of his business duds.

Me: Yeah, a lot like that. Clark Kent probably wished he could use his Superman laser vision to heat up leftovers.

Her: Ha! Maybe he did when he was alone. The human microwave.

Me: Did Superman have super powers when he was dressed as Clark Kent? I don't remember.

Her: I don't know. I think he had to be in uniform for it all to work right.

Me: The quick change in the phone booth, right? I wonder what he would have done today. There aren't any phone booths.

Her: True. I guess he would be a restroom changer.

Me: Now we're obsessing on Superman.

Her: And he's not even real. But we're pretending he is.

Me: What if he were real? What would you do if Superman walked into the Dive right now?

Her: I wouldn't do anything until I was sure it was him.

Me: My English professor wants us to say "it was he."

Her: That is so dumb.

Me: And so grammatical.

Her: It was he. Who talks that way?

Me: My English professor.

Her: Well, that's his obsession. And his problem. He's wrong, by the way.

Me: You mean it should be "it was him?"

Her: When everyone, and I mean everyone, says it that way, it is right. Grammar ought to be just a description of how people actually speak a language.

Me: God, you would fail his class in a day. We're obsessing again.

Her: On what?

Me: Well, grammar, I guess. Let's get back to Superman walking in right now.

Her: To make sure it was he—ha!—I would wait for him to do something superhuman.

Me: Like what?

Her: It wouldn't need to be much. He could just grab the top of this chair and reduce it to sawdust with his mighty grip. You know he can turn a lump of coal into a diamond, right?

Me: I read that somewhere. And would crunching a chair into sawdust prove that he was Superman?

Her: It would be enough for me. He wouldn't have to stop the Earth's rotation or fly around holding Lois Lane in his arms. Just a spoonful of sugar makes the medicine go down, as they say.

Me: I guess you're right. It wouldn't take much for Superman to show that he wasn't like any other human being.

Her: Have you read Dostoyevsky's *Brothers Karamazov*?

Me: Nope.

Her: Well, there's this one chapter where Jesus is being asked why he didn't use his supernatural powers to unhook himself from the cross and zap all the Romans.

Me: And the answer?

Her: He says, at least in the novel, that he didn't want to imprison people's minds.

Me: Say what?

Her: Imprison people's minds. If you and I ever saw something truly, obviously supernatural, we wouldn't ever be the same. Maybe we would be less than we were before.

Me: How so?

Her: We wouldn't be able to quit thinking about the Big Him, making us the Little Me's.

Me: Who's the Big Him?

Her: You know, like Superman. Once he had squeezed the top of a chair into sawdust or bored a laser hole through the wall, we couldn't help ourselves. We would obsess on how he did that.

Me: Yeah, the sawdust would suddenly turn into sacred stuff.

Her: Right. Sawdust worth a million dollars. Our minds would be imprisoned by his miraculous powers. We would realize how puny and helpless we were in comparison.
Me: I get it. Do you think Jesus did?

Her: I'm betting he didn't. If there was an actual human being named Jesus on a cross at Calvary, he was probably thinking about his pain, not about humanity's welfare.

Me: You don't buy the idea of one man saving all of mankind by dying?

Her: Not a very good script, would you say? No streaming media possibilities there. Imagine the pitch: "Man who thinks he is also God concludes that a bloody crucifixion will make up for all human wrongdoing past, present, and future and send everyone to a happy ending in heaven." I don't think the studios would buy it.

Me: You are going straight to hell.

Her: Ha! I don't believe in hell, either.

Me: What? You don't believe in a red guy with little horns and a long, pointed tail? Are you insane?

Her: Don't get me laughing. Put it this way. I would be very, very surprised if my first experience after death was hellfire licking at my toes.

Me: Not if you are cremated.

Her: I don't expect to be conscious. I said, after death.

Me: So, you probably don't believe in a soul?

Her: Nope. I think that death is the end. Finito.

Me: Unless Superman stepped in.

Her: That's exactly it. The idea of death scares the shit out of everyone. We are looking for some way out, a glimmer of hope. And we would find it in anyone who has authentic superhuman powers.

Me: However small.

Her: Yes, however small.

Me: So, Jesus could have made one of the spikes fly out of his pierced hand and stick some Roman guard in the forehead. That would have been enough to catch our attention?

Her: Absolutely. Great copy, as they say. The Bible writers would have jumped on it in a New York minute.

Me: The story of the crucifixion would have been recast as the Story of the Flying Spike. What do we remember of Moses? The miraculous parting of the Red Sea, of course.

Her: Yeah, I saw it in an old movie. Didn't look very realistic. But, doesn't it make you feel good just thinking about miracles? A basically nice guy like Jesus pulls out his supernatural skills and puts the whammy on his Roman tormentors. Liam Neeson stuff. "I have a unique set of skills . . ." That's all we want to see—someone who isn't stuck like the rest of us with mortality and 80 years, if we're lucky, before the Big Sleep.

Me: So, let me ask you. Do you think I have superhuman abilities?

Her: I've seen you do some things that I can't understand or explain. I guess you would say I am in awe of your ability to move bits of paper with your mind.

Me: So am I. But I can't do anything else, like leaping tall buildings at a single bound or even pushing a penny. At least so far.

Her: You think your abilities are evolving to something bigger?

Me: Not so far. Do you want them to?

Her: Hmm. Let's say you could snap your fingers and make a banana split magically appear right now on this table, maybe with two spoons. I think a hush would fall over the bar, don't you? It would certainly shut me up.

Me: Yeah, people would gather around to see it.

Her: For sure they would wonder what they had seen. Many wouldn't believe their eyes. Someone would shout, "Do it again."

Me: And I would do it again, just to prove that I could. Two banana splits.

Her: If so, you would instantly be on your way to becoming the most famous person on Earth.

Me: How so?

Her: Word would spread like wildfire that one Boston College undergraduate possessed demonstrable superhuman skills. You would be invited to the White House.

Me: And the President would ask me to do some . . . I wouldn't call them tricks, exactly.

Her: Not even approximately. That's the point. You are doing superhuman stuff, not illusions. And you would be able to do it over and over, on demand or on a whim.

Me: Unlike my efforts at moving my paper bits.

Her: Right. The only thing that keeps you from being the new Superman is the fact that you fail much more than you succeed with your mind-over-matter skills.

Me: So, if I could move bits of paper every time I wanted to, I would be world famous?

Her: Yes, God help you. But you would have to demonstrate your skills every time we—other human beings—wanted you to. It isn't a matter of what you choose to do. You would have to prove yourself over and over.

Me: Re-runs.

Her: Yep. And top scientists and other credible people at some point would have to weigh in to certify that you are not bound by the known laws of nature.

Me: Let me get the whole picture. I get validated by scientists and then?

Her: Then people drop everything they are doing to beat a path to your door.

Me: But all I have to offer is bits of paper scooting a foot or two across a tabletop.

Her: That's enough. Superman and the sawdust, right? It doesn't take much supernatural ability to imprison the minds of every living and dying human being on Earth.

Me: You're saying they would obsess on me?

Her: Big time. Like thinking about a banana split. Men and women everywhere would think of you the first moment they wake up and dream about you when they sleep.

Me: The moving bits of paper are that interesting?

Her: Of course not. They are boring. But getting above and beyond the natural order of things—that's incredible. You would be worshipped like a god. You would be a god.

Me: With a capital 'G' or a lowercase 'g'? There have been a lot of the latter. Olympus, King Tut, and all that.

Her: I would say a capital 'G.' I mean, the Christian deity doesn't have a very spiffy record of showing up when needed, correct? People talk about communicating with God in times of need, but it's a one-way conversation. No one is picking up the phone at the other end of our calls.

Me: But people swear that God has helped them. Some of the Superbowl champions thanked God for their win.

Her: Or for protecting them from injury. Or for allowing the best team to triumph. Or for watching over their families and fans. Even for keeping a knee-brace from slipping. You get the idea--pure wish fulfillment and nothing demonstrable. Just business as usual, with no verifiable pinch of supernatural spice.

Me: But I would have a chance at the capital 'G'?

Her: Absolutely. You just have to be reliably supernatural. It isn't the size of your skill. It's the skill itself—the proof that you are outside of nature and natural laws. That's all it takes to be God.

Me: And I wouldn't have to save anyone?

Her: Why? You've already saved everyone by giving them hope.

Me: Hope for what?

Her: Hope that someone flew over the cuckoo's nest.

Me: But they didn't. I did.

Her: They don't need to. They've given up on discovering superhuman powers of their own. Enough that you've got these powers and can show them repeatedly to doubters.

Me: So, I spend my time just moving bits of paper?

Her: All around the world, over and over. People will pay anything to be in your presence and to see the only certifiable display of superhuman skills on Earth.

Me: And they get what from this?

Her: As I said, a little hope. You have broken through the closed loop of natural laws. You have opened the door of possibility to a way out of nature, with all its unpredictability and tragedy. Every time people see one of your paper bits moving by the power of your mind alone, they let themselves hope a little more that there is a God in heaven and on Earth.

Me: And am I that God?

Her: You tell me. Maybe you are a representative of God, like his or her son or something. But the point is that you are all humanity has to go on—the only verifiable spark of the divine in human life. Until the home office reveals its address, the traveling salesman—you—are our only sign that maybe there's a way out of the death sentence we're under.

Me: I wouldn't be saving anyone from death.

Her: True. But people would ask you to save them.

Me: How do you mean?

Her: You would be the Saint of Boston College. People would come by the thousands to touch the hem of your clothing, maybe have you lay a hand on them or their sick children.

Me: Touching my clothing or having the touch of my hand wouldn't change a thing. All I can do is move bits of paper.

Her: Superhuman ability. That's the key. Moving paper bits is just the tip of the iceberg. People will imagine what lies beneath the surface. Superman just had to make a little sawdust, right? He didn't have to do anything grand to make us believe.

Me: Sounds like beggars can't be choosers.

Her: Exactly. Mankind has zilch in the tank when it comes to escaping the mighty mousetrap of nature—so they will grasp at straws or, in your case, bits of paper. Any port in a storm.

Me: Let me get this straight. All I have to do if I want godlike attention is to perfect my paper routine so that I can do it repeatably, no matter what the conditions?

Her: That would do it. So far, people don't believe in your abilities because you misfire so often. Jesus wouldn't have gained much notoriety if he had succeeded in changing water to wine at only one in ten weddings. Go big or go home. Just do it. That's what humanity craves.

Me: Someone could get trampled when thousands of people are beating a path to their door.

Her: Good point. There's a reason so many religions feature worshippers eating their God in some form. Communion, for example.

Me: Translating, I could get crushed, destroyed, by people wanting to see me do my thing.

Her: It's possible. Being supernatural in your abilities comes with risks.

Me: That's probably why Superman needed a bulletproof skin. And he could always fly away to his Fortress of Solitude at the North Pole.

Her: You would need something like that. Protection from the masses. A reliable retreat from their needs. Their constant clamor for another demonstration of your skills would eat you alive.

Me: Maybe I would have demonstrations only once a month. They could be broadcast internationally or streamed on Netflix.

Her: And repeatedly certified as authentic. Don't forget that part. A lot of tricksters are out there trying to dominate the wills and wealth of humanity. A panel of renowned scientists, maybe with backup from presidents and potentates, would have to speak up on your behalf at each demonstration, assuring people that you are what you claim to be: a person with supernatural skills.

Me: Would once a month be enough?

Her: You decide. If you leave it up to the man or woman on the street, they will want demonstrations 24/7. How often does a prisoner want to see a gleam of sunshine through the bars?

Me: You've given me a lot to think about. The takeaway for me is that getting consistent with my paper bits routine is kinda dangerous. I've avoided the limelight so far because I fail much more than I succeed.

Her: Right. You've given people grounds to doubt you. Only consistent supernatural demonstrations can turn skeptics into worshippers.

Me: I certainly am not seeking worshippers. Who wants to be worshipped?

Her: Duh, like every movie star and every politician? Think of what it must be like to have millions of people saying that you are just divine.

Me: Again, not me. Maybe it's my Asperger's. I don't want public adulation.

Her: Comes with the territory. You can't be supernatural and hide your candle under a basket, which is what you've been doing so far. When you can predictably move even the smallest of things on command, you will have to decide whether to be a hermit or an icon. There's no middle ground.

Me: So, I can't be a gentleman farmer, ploughing and planting a little here and there as I choose?

Her: No way. Once word gets out that there's a supernatural fox in the chicken coop, your destiny is fixed. Everyone will want a piece of you.

Me: There's that eating metaphor again. Yuck!

Her: If you don't want to be the Biggest Fucking Deal in human history, don't go there—just keep futzing around with your abilities as a whacky, unreliable hobby. Then people can dismiss you as interesting but crazy.

Me: Is that how you think of me? Interesting but crazy?

Her: I think of you as interesting and lovable. But I'm glad I'm not you. I wouldn't want to face your choices.

Me: If I do get my act together and get stamped as the only validated, predictable source of the supernatural on Earth, how would you treat me?

Her: Like Superman. I would be your Lois Lane.

Me: But no worship?

Her: More than worship. Adoration.

Chapter Eight
"If I Did It"

I n 2006 HarperCollins announced its plans to publish O.J. Simpson's *If I Did It: Confessions of the Killer,* a hypothetical account of how the murders of Ron Goldman and Nicole Simpson could have occurred. Public outcry over the prospect that O.J. would profit from his crimes as described in a civil judgment against him led to O.J.'s bankruptcy ruling in 2007. The court assigned rights to the book to the Goldman family. They published it as Simpson's true confession, at least in their view.

I have nothing to confess regarding my psychokinetic abilities, such as they are. But I must admit that I often wonder if I am myself a dupe of some arcane "trick" of physics, especially because, as I've said, my success with bits of paper occurs only about ten percent of the time. On one hand, why would I fail so often if I had some trick up my sleeve? On the other hand, what better deception than to fake failure as proof that I'm not controlling my exhibition of mind over matter?

These aren't the kinds of speculations one discusses with parents. In fact, I've never shown my prowess with paper bits to my parents. Maybe it was time to do so.

"Can we talk?" I blurted out after dinner with Mom and Dad during Christmas vacation of my junior year.

These words had a galvanizing effect on my parents. I could see shades of terror playing across their faces: Does he have an STD? Is he coming out and, if so, as what? Has he failed out of college? And the worst horror of all for families everywhere: Has he decided to go to medical school?

They motioned me into the livingroom, where all substantive conversations in my family seemed to take place.

"Well," I began, "I've gotten a reputation of sorts as a magician in my fraternity."

"Magician?" my mother said weakly, perhaps thinking that I was gender-fluid.

"Magician," I repeated. "I really don't know if I am doing a magic trick or if I have genuine mental powers."

My father leaned forward and motioned me with his hand to fill in the details. I told them the short version of my on-and-off ability to move paper bits. Once they had gauged the nature of my secret, my parents both slumped back with a sigh of relief. "We thought this was something serious," my father exhaled.

"It is serious," I protested. "I'm stuck with some kind of power that I don't understand. Dad, how would you feel if you concentrated on the TV clicker across the room and made it automatically fly into your hand?"

He shrugged. "I would feel wonderful."

My mother frowned toward me. "You have the ability to make the TV clicker fly through the air?"

"No," I explained, "just paper bits. And only once in a while. I can't do my magic or whatever on command. Maybe it's genetic. Did either of you ever have unexplained mental powers?"

My parents looked blankly at one another, then at me. "I was an early reader," my mother said. "And your father can remember license plates and phone numbers. Is that what you mean?"

"Not exactly," I said, not wanting to rain on their parade of amazing mental skills. "You have never moved anything using just your mind?"

"My bowels," my father joked. Mom rolled her eyes.

"I'm serious," I pressed on. "This thing is driving me crazy. There has to be some explanation other than truly superhuman powers. I don't feel superhuman."

"You don't look superhuman," my mother reassured.

My father stroked his chin. "Can you show us this magic?"

I welcomed the opportunity and attempted to make paper bits move across the livingroom coffee table. No cigar. My parents watched my five or six attempts with mixed expressions of patience and pity on their faces.

"Maybe you should talk to Uncle Jacob," my father finally said.

"Uncle Jacob?" I vaguely remembered him as a stubble-bearded retiree who visited once every three or four years, usually for a holiday meal. Why Uncle Jacob?

"He was a magician, you know," my father explained. "He could tell you how a magician would create the illusion you describe." He paused. "Assuming, of course, it isn't an ability that is . . . uh, superhuman." He smiled.

"Or Satanic," I stuck in. "My roommate's mother says it might be the work of the devil."

"We don't believe in the devil," my mother corrected. She looked at my father. "Do we?" He smirked 'no, dear.'

I didn't usually agree with any of my father's suggestions, but this one had legs. "Uncle Jacob. That's a good idea," I admitted. "Can you put us in touch?"

"He's staying overnight with us this coming Friday," my father said. "For turkey. Sit down and talk with him."

* * * * *

Uncle Jacob was more approachable than I had remembered. He said he was glad to chat with me about what I was experiencing. We sat across from one another in the livingroom, with my parents out of the room, but probably listening from a distance.

"Watch this," Jacob said, playing a silver dollar back and forth across his knuckles before making it disappear into the air. "There's an explanation to where it went, but a magician never shows how the trick is done."

"Why not?" I asked, anticipating that he wouldn't be willing to share any so-called trick that explained my mental abilities.

"Because the audience doesn't really want to know," Jacob replied. "Once they know how a trick is done, the wonder and delight evaporates. The audience comes to a magician for awe, not explanations. Where else in their daily lives can they find something that seems to be miraculous?"

I pondered his question for a moment. "Is it possible that I'm doing a trick without realizing it?" I explained to him in detail exactly what I was able to do, or not, with paper bits.

He took in my information without comment or visible reaction. "Well," he said, after I had finished my info dump, "you have a few things going for you."

I didn't understand. "Going for me?"

"I mean," he said, "you are doing things that an experienced magician would do."

"Such as?" I asked.

"Three things in particular," he answered, letting the silver dollar play across his knuckles again. "First, you said you move the paper bits toward you. That eliminates blowing air from your mouth. You would be surprised how many illusions depend just on a subtle stream of air. And moving the bits toward you is striking. Beginning magicians make everything fly toward the audience as a form of misdirection."

I nodded. "And number two?"

"Second," he said, "your bits of paper move at different speeds. That eliminates a big magnet under the table--you know, a powerful magnetic field interacting with some iron filings in the paper bits. If you were using a large magnet strapped to your knee, the bits of paper would tend to move together at one speed."

"I get it," I said. "And the third thing?"

"You play dumb," he said. "That's what some of the best magicians do. They act as if they, too, are befuddled by the illusion. They don't act like the only guy in the room who knows the trick, that sort of thing. Nothing smug. By their words and reactions, they pretend to say 'OMG!' along with the audience. That's what you're doing, and very well."

I was silent for a moment. "But I'm not pretending. I don't think I am doing a trick."

Jacob rubbed his hands. "OK. Let's consider some other possibilities. The individual movement of paper bits could be explained by invisible threads connected to each piece."

"Invisible threads?" I echoed.

"Yes. Tricky little items, for sale at any magic shop. Each thread is incredibly thin, like one strand from a spider's web. Most illusions having to do with objects floating in space or moving at the magician's command are based on an invisible thread. In your case, you could make the individual paper bits move at various speeds simply by connecting an invisible thread to each one. You stick an invisible thread onto a paper bit, using a dab of magician's putty. Then, when the illusion is over, you subtly peal the putty and attached thread off each paper bit as you hand them to the audience for inspection."

I knew I hadn't used invisible threads, but Jacob's alternate explanations interested me. They were certainly more logical than the idea of superhuman powers.

"Or," he said, "there's the art of using static electricity."

Say what? I had been accused by frat brothers of using static electricity, but I didn't know why or how.

"Static electricity," Jacob continued, "has been used for centuries as a hidden means of exciting motion in small items such as paper bits, toothpicks, that kind of thing. The magician charges his body with a positive electric charge—no equipment necessary, just a quick rub with a piece of wool or silk fabric. The paper bits, or whatever, are negatively charged, or 'grounded,' by their contact with the tabletop. Works even when the objects are in a jar."

"And the static electricity does what?" I asked.

"You've seen this effect when you're unpacking a box with Styrofoam shipping peanuts. They dance around your fingers, all due to the interaction of the positive charge in your hands and the negative charge of the peanuts. Same effect with paper bits. They appear to move toward your hands in the same way the Styrofoam peanuts do. Looks like they are moving on their own, but they are just responding to the physics of static electricity."

"Interesting," I said. "So, that could explain why my success rate is so low?"

"It could," Jacob replied, "especially if you aren't being careful to keep your hands from grounding out their positive charge. Even the slightest touch to the tabletop or other surface will neutralize the effect of static electricity."

I played over in my mind the possibility that I was inadvertently using static electricity to move my bits of paper. Had I rubbed my pants legs together under the table to create a charge? Unlikely, I thought, since I had worn gym shorts on more than one paper-moving occasion. And I wasn't in the habit of briskly rubbing my hands together. That would have been obvious to my audience—and to me.

Jacob interrupted. "Of course," he laughed, "it all depends how much money you have. Famous magicians like David Copperfield spend many thousands of dollars on hi-tech apparatus that you would never suspect or discover."

"Hi-tech?" I asked. I wanted to hear more.

"It's the untold story behind most big illusions you see on TV and in Las Vegas," he answered. "Take mind-reading acts, for example. The magician is in the audience, supposedly sending mental messages or whatever to his blindfolded assistant seated on the stage. But no-one thinks to look at the chair the assistant is sitting on. The truth is that the chair costs about $1200—look on line, you'll find one--and is capable, through hidden wires and batteries, of delivering a vibration or slight shock to the assistant sitting in the chair. The magician in the audience can control these electric signals by subtly touching his ring or other broadcasting unit."

"So, the assistant feels a particular series of vibrations or little shocks and makes a correct guess?"

"Numbers, colors, addresses, shoe size, you name it. But it's not a guess. It's just reading a code worked out in advance with the magician."

"What if I inspected the chair?" I asked.

"You wouldn't find anything," Jacob replied. "That's why it costs $1200 or more. Looks just like an ordinary folding chair."

"So," I paused. "If"—I suddenly felt too much like O.J—"if I were doing a trick, what kind of hi-tech apparatus could be used to move my paper bits?"

"Depends on your budget," Jacob responded. "On the cheap side, you could wire the inside of your desk or tabletop to generate a static charge. On the more expensive side, you could use servo motors to slightly tip your surface at the same time that everything else immediately in view around it was slightly lowered by motors. Gravity does the rest—anything placed on the desk or tabletop will appear to slide toward you. Works great on TV. Or you could engineer a strong field of electrical charge, maybe radiated from the curtains or wall. The field is beamed out to your performance area. Tesla let electricity dance off his fingertips. Using an external electric field, you could do your trick on any surface. For a few thousand bucks, you could retrofit the inside of your desk or tabletop with a series of hidden magnets that drive anything on the surface—anything containing a trace of iron. That's why you see magicians use tacks, paperclips, and hairpins so often. All are perfect for movement that appears to be psychokinetic. The trick is just magnetic—and expensive."

He had said the magic word. Psychokinetic. "Have you ever seen any verified psychokinetic phenomenon?" I asked.

"Nope," he shrugged. "Not in almost fifty years as a practicing magician. I've seen illusions that I can't explain, but only because the magician wasn't in the habit of revealing what he or she had spent a lot of time and money perfecting. Actual psychokinesis? Never."

High time, of course, for a demonstration of my powers. Jacob folded his arms and sat back to observe my act.

I tried. I really tried. It just wasn't working. After half an hour of watching my face turn red and sweaty from concentrated effort, Jacob called a halt: "Fine, fine," he said, "don't strain yourself. I get the general idea. And," he added, without sarcasm, "I do believe that your trick works sometimes. Maybe I have given you some ideas of how it is happening."

I thanked him and told him I would be in touch once I figured out what was going on.

* * * * *

Lying in bed that night I reviewed the possibilities. I knew I had not invested thousands of dollars in any hi-tech apparatus, and the desktop in my room was certainly not wired for magnetic or static electrical effects. There were no rustling curtains near my desk, nothing to generate a field of charge. Absolutely no hidden threads running from my fingertips or pants leg to the paper bits.

Innocent, your honor! If the bits fit, you must acquit! I knew now from Jacob how it could be done. But, on my honor as a non-magician, I didn't do it.

Unless, of course, I was crazy—"crazy," the charge used most often to indict those claiming to have superhuman powers. If I were locked in some annoying alternate reality, I would be the last person to recognize or understand my situation. I thought about Einstein's undersized brain, the EPR Paradox, and the theory of relativity. I suppose the very best con men are those who believe their own con.

I fell asleep, dreaming fitfully about a roaring lion walking about, seeking whom he may devour. The lion could talk. He was saying, "I am innocent, your honor."

Chapter Nine
Opportunity Knocks

'm coming up on 23 years old. Halfway to 46. Unimaginable.

At this point, I have my own apartment and a bearable job doing coding for Electronic Arts. I'm not a game guy, which is probably what makes me valuable to EA. Gamers can't see beyond their own favorite features from other games—and they code accordingly.

I don't have any favorite features. My boss calls my coding "very innovative." That's because I don't know better.

My roommate, with benefits, is Viola. You remember her. She's a first-year accountant with KPMG. Smart young woman. She suspects that our relationship will move to engagement within a year or two. She may be right.

In the meantime, I object to the idea of an engagement ring. Pardon this Asperger's moment—it will pass. No, I haven't discussed ring prices with Viola. I'm on my own life support here. Think about it: a diamond ring is a huge, unnecessary expense for anyone just starting out. And the tab for a traditional wedding is a hell of a burden for parents, just when they thought they had written the last, big college check. One day of wedding fru-fru costs upwards of $50,000, which I assume her parents and mine will split. Add another $5,000 when she says "yes to the dress." What a racket! I guess we could elope, if I want to condemn myself to a lifetime of regrets from my spouse— "never had a real wedding." I can hear it now.

Given these stormy financial seas dead ahead, the unexpected phone call from Madame Li's business manager was welcome.

"Madame Li wants to follow up on your act. You remember, you met with her about a year ago in Minneapolis?"

My stomach was flipping. Of course I remember.

He sounded excited. "We have a bit of an opportunity for you. I'm calling to give you the quick sketch. I'll send you all the details by email. OK?"

"Yes, certainly." My voice shook a little.

"You've watched Madame Li's TV show, right? Well, the producer has a new feature in mind that could involve you."

I'm listening—like a bat.

He continued. "There would be a short segment at the end of the show where we briefly introduce three new magicians and their acts on video. The audience votes on which one we should invite to appear as a full-fledged guest on the show."

"A video?" My voice was higher than I intended. I swallowed, thinking back to the amateurish video clip I had left with Madame Li.

"Yeah, just iPhone quality. Nothing too slick. The idea is to show new magicians at the very beginning of their careers. The video can be rough around the edges. Preferable, in fact. Madame Li likes the video you left with her."

Good to know. The quivers in my voice were easing.

"Madame Li and Benson have watched it several times. Great stuff. And just the right length—about a minute." He let a beat of silence fall. "This is a paying gig, even if the audience doesn't choose you. $5000 for the right to show your video. And much more if you're chosen."

I said a silent Hallelujah. Five thousand dollars! My wish-list flashed like a Las Vegas neon: a new laptop and a pair of Allbirds shoes and maybe a decent mattress. No doubt Viola would have things she wanted to say "yes" to.

We wrapped up our phone call and, true to his word, an email arrived shortly thereafter with all the details of the deal. I didn't have to travel to Minneapolis, at least not yet. And I didn't have to create a new video starring Me and the Bits. Thank God.

Speaking of which, there's news to share. I have been so tied up with my EA job and life with Viola that I haven't exercised my mind muscles lately. Not for six months or so. That's an eternity for superhuman powers. Even Superman would go flabby with six months off.

This hiatus wouldn't matter if I struck out with Madame Li's audience. The $5000 would be paid just for their use of the video, according to the yet-unsigned contract. But what if the audience chose me?

Although I hadn't played with my paper bits lately, I guessed that my batting average of one success in ten tries had not improved and maybe had grown worse. No matter how much money I would earn if I were chosen for the TV show, "earn" was the operative word. I couldn't just swing and miss—"oops, there. That's all, folks!" The small print in the contract I received from Madame Li committed me, if selected by the audience, to a full five minutes of on-air "magic entertainment," not embarrassing failure.

I decided to call Madame Li. We had connected, I felt, when I visited Minneapolis. She knew from the beginning about my projectile dysfunction. Paper bits weren't exactly projectiles, but I liked the phrase.

I put off making the call for several days. I needed to play it over (and over) in my head. When I eventually reached Madame Li, she was understanding about my hesitation.

"I get it," she assured me. "We can package your act any way you want. The mystery of whether you will succeed may even be a plus. Our backup would be another video, this one showing you doing your act right on my palms, just as before. You could work with that, right?"

I answered "yes" while thinking "maybe" to myself. The truth was that practice didn't make perfect when it came to superhuman powers. Perhaps that is why I had neglected my paper bits lately. I got tired of missing the mark after, sometimes, twenty or more tries in row. And I worried that my skills were evaporating.

I couldn't sleep after talking to Madame Li. I woke up at 2 am, with that damn lion proclaiming his innocence in my dreams. Viola felt me stir and asked what was wrong. "It's like dominoes," I told her. "If I take the $5000 and they put my video on TV, there's no stopping the train from that point on. The contract commits me to appear on her TV show if I'm chosen by the audience. And how would that go? You know I'm not reliable at all in being able to do my thing on command."

Viola was a good listener. I could always depend on her for a well-reasoned perspective. Just what I needed in the wee hours.

"Tom," she whispered, pulling herself out of sleep, "you don't have to sign anything. How do you really feel about being famous?"

I rolled to face her. I think I was facing her. It was dark.

"The money attracts me more than the fame," I answered. "We could be wealthy within a year or two, but the price would be a lot of pressure to perform. One high-profile failure and people would be laughing at me. Just like Don Quixote on the M.I.T. broadcast."

"What would happen if you said no to the whole thing?"

"Nothing," I answered. "Madame Li probably has a list of a hundred or more aspiring magicians who want to strut their stuff on TV. The money would be nice, but we won't starve. We both have pretty good jobs."

She sensed I was calming down. "Sleep on it," she murmured, pulling the covers under her chin. "We'll talk more in the morning."

* * * * *

The morning in question was Saturday. Viola was up at some ungodly hour and messing with her laptop.

"We need a spreadsheet," she called out as I stumbled toward the coffee. "You can put down all the pluses and minuses."

"Of what?" I wasn't awake.

"The question of whether to let Madame Li use your video. You know, the contract. $5000. Maybe more."

"Uh . . . OK," I hesitated. This was definitely an accountant's path to making important decisions, not mine. She pressed a key on her laptop and a large, blank spreadsheet appeared on our livingroom TV. We plopped next to one another on the couch to begin our work.

"Do you want to do the pluses first or the minuses?" Viola asked.

I shrugged. "Let's just take them as they come," I said. "I don't want to organize this thing too rigidly."

There was something in those words that caused offense. She rolled her eyes. "OK. Random order. Whatever."

I don't recall the exact sequence in which the pluses and minuses appeared on the spreadsheet. Viola and I talked for more than an hour on a few of the items.

Here's the result.

PLUS: We could really use the $5000. Viola had these funds earmarked in advance for wedding expenses, which she disguised behind the phrase "our future." I had the funds earmarked, too, but thought it better not to mention the road bike I had in mind. I nodded at the phrase "our future" and let it go at that.

MINUS: My struggling reputation as a Wunderkind would be scotched forever if I failed to perform on TV. Did I really care?, Viola asked. Yes. The thought of having millions of TV viewers laughing at me didn't sit well.

MINUS: Even if my mind powers worked on the TV show, the future thereafter was unpredictable. How would the world react if Madame Li said something like, "I believe Tom is demonstrating true psychokinesis. This isn't magic or an act. This is the real McCoy, maybe for the first time in human history. I stake my reputation on it."

That kind of news would rocket around the planet. I would be swept up into god-knows-what. I didn't want to be a guru or shaman. I could stand modest fame but not mega-fame. Where would I put "supernatural powers" on my resume?

PLUS: Our college friends who mocked my mental powers would have their come-uppance. I could hear them now: "Shit, that Tom guy was for real! Can you believe it? That putz in our fraternity! Even Madame Li says that Tom has genuine superhuman powers." I would do my part to rub it in on Facebook, Twitter, and Instagram. Revenge is best served electronically.

MINUS: My relationship with Viola could change for the worse, as kings, queens, presidents, and potentates invited me for performances. How would Viola feel as my lady-in-waiting?

PLUS: A lot of smart people would be alerted to my superpowers. Maybe these people could help me understand my mental abilities.

MINUS: A lot of smart people would be alerted to my superpowers. These people would want to test my abilities endlessly. If I said 'no' to perpetual testing, what would that say to the world? Curious minds want to know.

MINUS: The vast majority of movies and TV shows about supernatural powers center on an evil Pentagon seeking to weaponize the abilities of the hapless psychic. Would this turn out to be true in my case? Being a weapon struck me as an odd career path. I hadn't seen it listed on any of the job sites.

PLUS: I could provide financially for Viola and my parents. Viola and I could get a dog. (She wants a cat.) My fee schedule for performances could be dialed up to stratospheric levels. I would be the LeBron James of the miraculous and profitable.

MINUS: I glimpsed from my lunch with Johnson's mother and her religious group that there was palpable danger for me from these nut-jobs. If the word spread among the fringe element of world religions that I was an agent of the Bad Guy, by whatever name, I would have to live behind high walls, just as Salmon Rushdie did when faced by a fatwa. High walls do a prison make.

MINUS: This item was a bit silly, I thought, but Viola wanted it on the list. How could we have a cat and also travel around the world? Who would feed it and exercise it? Cats don't travel well. Could we really tell the Queen of England that I couldn't accommodate her request for a performance because we have a cat? And, I hastened to remind Viola, the dog-cat issue hadn't yet been decided. Dogs kennel better than cats.

PLUS: I would have personal satisfaction in displaying my skills to an appreciative public. Hiding one's candle under a basket only leads to house fires. That's a metaphor.

MINUS: Viola wanted to key in "BIG MINUS" for this item. I grant that it is significant, but not moreso than the other pluses and minuses. Our wedding plans would have to scale up in direct correlation to my world-wide fame. Do you think Princess Di's wedding was a big affair? Imagine the hoopla for the wedding of the only bonafide supernaturalist in all of human history! Where would the wedding take place? Certainly not in our local First Presbyterian church. Ditto for the birth of our children. Would they inherit the super-gene? Viola worries about the children's names—Elektra? Zeus? Woden? And what burden of expectation would they face from the world as I eventually, with the touch of time, prove to be mortal? Would my kids be under the gun to carry my torch? That's a mixed metaphor.

PLUS or MINUS, depending on your perspective: What's best for humanity? I know that question has a Bernie Sanders ring to it. But, seriously, what would almost 8 billion people gain or lose if I went public with my superhuman powers? I should reduce that number— about half of all human beings now on Earth will never make or receive a telephone call, or so I'm told by my cellular service provider. On the plus side, the remaining population of the Earth stands to gain some light at the end of the tunnel (yes, another metaphor). They would have verified evidence that there is more to our existence than birth, 80 years of life if we're lucky, and death. They would find hope in the idea that somewhere, somehow, one human being (*moi*) has succeeded in shaking off the surly bonds of Earth to demonstrate superhuman powers.

On the MINUS side, the notoriety of my superpowers could give birth to an immense wave of spiritualism not unlike the Great Awakening in the 1730s and '40s. I was uncomfortable with the idea that people would seek God, heaven, and a full tank of religiosity all because I could move bits of paper with my mind. I recalled the Grand Inquisitor's question to Jesus: Why didn't you do a miracle and come down off the cross? And his answer: even a spark of the miraculous in human existence has the potential to grow into an uncontrollable forest fire.

The supposed image of Jesus's face on a toasted cheese sandwich brought thousands of curious pilgrims to the door of Florida's Diana Duyser in 2004—and $28,000 to her bank account when she sold the sandwich ten years later. That's what happens when minds freed to think by the scientific revolution—even freed to think about a heedless universe instead of a caring Mother Nature-- devolve into minds imprisoned by the miraculous, the mysterious, and the supernatural. I didn't want to fuel the fires of Mothman, Roswell, and Jonestown. (I'm not venting here about insects, UFOs, or Koolaid.) I do recognize the kernel of truth in the idea that the slave creates the master. I would stand in danger of losing myself as mankind re-made me in the image of their own desperate needs.

Heady stuff. Steady huff. You choose.

* * * * *

The list was probably longer. I get a bit dizzy thinking about the endless pros and cons arising from the not-so-simple act of moving bits of paper.

Of course, Viola and I couldn't simply sum the list and go with the majority opinion. The Anna Karenina Effect makes clear that a single in-your-face MINUS can be more important than a host of PLUSES. It's rare, I think, that the opposite is true—one major PLUS overcoming a host of MINUSES in human affairs. Maybe the judges in the Miss America Contest would disagree.

The eventual decision wasn't made easily, nor has it been cast in granite. There's always a Rocky IV, V, or VI lurking around the corner. My ultimate decision about what to do with Madame Li's contract in my hands and, by extension, my predictable future fame, could change tomorrow. I know that Madame Li's TV offer isn't good forever. She will move on to the next guy, even though he or she isn't unique at all in the annals of human history.

And the verdict?

Epilogue

I finish this unexpectedly long journal entry some 20 years later. At this point in time, I find myself comfortable as an upper level manager, still with Electronic Arts, but no longer coding. Viola, beautiful being, has proven to be my soulmate in every way. She is the mother of two exquisite children, Sean and Christy, born a year apart and now half-way through college. No medical school in sight, thank you.

In the top drawer of my office desk sit three bits of paper pleading for play. I air them out on my desktop every so often, but can't bring myself to make them move. What's to be gained? I opted long ago, in my twenties, to forego universal fame for local contentment. The MINUS category won out over the PLUS potentials. If I had been blessed—cursed—with consistency in my mental abilities, perhaps I would have made a different choice.

But that's all in the past. Neither of my children has inherited the super-gene, if indeed it rests in my DNA. I've told them the story of my paper bits on more than one occasion. Their interest in my tale is, shall we say, polite and inattentive. I sense that they chalk it up to fuzzy, revisionist history from a by-gone era. When the topic came up a few months ago, Sean conceded that he "wished he had been there to see the paper bits move." I was tempted, of course, to show him my skills then and there.

But to what end? If I failed, he would pat me on the shoulder and say, "I love you anyway, Dad." If I succeeded, he would be condemned to pursue my lifelong search of trying to explain the undeniable but unfathomable. I would rather have him pass his college classes.

Viola is glad that I am thoroughly hers, not the world's. In the last couple decades, she and I have seen and discussed the rise and fall of world saviors. I choose not to run and, if elected, I will not serve.

Occasionally, she and I take in a magic show. We've even traveled to Minneapolis to see The Amazing Lily Li's performances, still in her mother's theatre. She is her mother's daughter, committed to flawless technique and fully prepared to rip the heart out of any magician who claims authentic superhuman skills.

At magicians' performances, Viola often asks me how a particular trick is done. I've become a student of magic. I share freely with my wife what I know. Usually, however, I have no idea. What you see is a craft, I assure her. It isn't supernatural. We will never find out how the magician did the trick.

We will never find out . . . . That's the sum of my life experience to date. In the most important matters of life and death, we will never find out. In our comfortable chairs, in our well-appointed homes, in our warm beds, we live in blissful ignorance of ultimate questions starting with How and Why. We will never find out. It would take a miracle to change that reality. I'm fearful of miracles and miracle-makers. I was one.

I wrote to Madame Li yesterday. She is well into her 70s and toddles on as the main mentor and enthusiastic fan of The Amazing Lily Li. She and I have stayed in touch, never discussing my one-off video of moving paper bits from so many years ago. I believe she has chalked it up to damn good magic, by which she means excellent technique. Truth be told, I haven't crossed that bridge. I continue to believe that I had, maybe still have, unexplained mental powers. We will never know. That's for the best.

One upsetting footnote: I reached a moment ago to close my journal, literally and figuratively, and with this final entry to put to rest any lingering fascination or obsession with my mental powers. As I reached to flip the journal shut once and for all, the cover quivered slightly before I had a chance to touch it. Then the journal slowly, elegantly, proceeded shut all by itself.

I kid you not. But I've said that all along.